ESCAPE FROM THE CLAN

by
Gregory Marcel

Gotham Books

30 N Gould St.
Ste. 20820, Sheridan, WY 82801
https://gothambooksinc.com/

Phone: 1 (307) 464-7800

© 2024 *Gregory Marcel*. All rights reserved.

No part of this book may be reproduced, stored in a retrieval system, or transmitted by any means without the written permission of the author.

Published by Gotham Books (May 1, 2024)

ISBN: 979-8-88775-805-3 (P)
ISBN: 979-8-88775-806-0 (E)

Because of the dynamic nature of the Internet, any web addresses or links contained in this book may have changed since publication and may no longer be valid.

The views expressed in this work are solely those of the author and do not necessarily reflect the views of the publisher, and the publisher hereby disclaims any responsibility for them.

To Mom

Roger

CHAPTER 1

THE NOOSE

I half-slid, half-crawled out of my semi comfortable but warm bed, and quietly headed for the window, still groggy with sleep. Tucked away in the corner of my room, the window was the only thing that I didn't question about the construction of the house. An eternity seemed to pass before I awkwardly reached my intended destination. It was well after one o'clock in the morning. I was pleased that I hadn't awakened anyone. The window was wide open. The sliding window was in decent working condition, with the screen on the outside. When the lights were off, you could see outside without being seen in the room.

As I began to shut the window, I heard voices. They were strong but muffled. Alarmed, I snapped fully awake and lay flat on the floor, motionless. I was thankful that I had cleaned up my room earlier in the day. Who knows what I'd be lying on if I hadn't taken the time to straighten up the place. The voices were becoming more distinct. "So this is where the nigger lives. What do you think, boys? Should we torch this shack?"

"Not now, Bob. Let's let the boy think he's getting away with something, then we'll make our move. He'll learn about messing with our women." Frozen with fear, I couldn't move. Questions raced through my mind: What if they torch the house? What if they come back? How long will they stay out there? Then I smelled cigarette smoke, liquor, and gasoline! My heart was pounding so hard that I thought the people outside could hear it. Suddenly, over the sound of my pulsating heart, I heard someone coming down the hall toward my room. The window was still open, so I had to break out of the paralyzing fear that had seized me and get to the door; I needed to get there before someone turned on the lights in my room. With all my strength, I forced myself to crawl to my bedroom door and intercept whoever it was. To my surprise, the hallway was empty. Motionless, I was frozen in position on my hands and knees, in utter disbelief!

I looked at my watch—it was almost two o'clock now—and here I was trembling and afraid. I could still hear the voices outside. A little calmer now, I crawled back to the window. They were talking real low—so low that I couldn't make out what was being said. I lay there for forty-five minutes, and then, finally, I poked my head up and looked out the window. To my astonishment they were gone. I could see a group of about a dozen people, maybe a few hundred feet down the block, walking away from my house. I relaxed somewhat, and then I assessed the situation.

I knew from experience that messing around with those fine-ass white women would get me in trouble. Now while I was not a particularly handsome man, I could hold my own with women of any race, but to me white women embodied the American ideal. I felt that women of color were exotic or beautiful, but I had to admire the white women's intuition—it went hand in hand with the complicated way of life in America. I can't count how many times my white female friends either bailed me out of a tight spot or gave me some timely advice. But somebody wanted to get rid of me and in the worst possible way. I began to calm down. Reflecting on the situation helped me to stand up. Once I did, I had to lean up against the wall and gather my thoughts. There was no way I could go back to sleep now. Even though it was cold out this morning, the chill would do me some good.

My fiancée, Casey Balkner, was a Catholic Caucasian from Philadelphia, who had moved to Washington state about eighteen months ago. I met her while I was doing some errands for my boss. Casey turned out to be a wonderful woman. She was something of a sympathizer with black Americans, but, for the most part, she didn't get too close. Through past experience, she knew that if you played with fire, you might get burned. I loved her for that—the ability to appreciate the disillusionment that blacks faced. Yet she had learned in Philly the danger of trying to befriend someone who faced discrimination constantly; this discrimination caused the sufferer to lash out at anyone trying to get close, whether white or black.

Yes, Casey played it cool, but once she figured out that you could deal with life, she was a real sweetheart. Casey was an average size, short with a bit of fleshiness around the hips. She had dark hair, falling just below her neck, but what stood out about Casey was her disarming, chubby-cheeked face. She had beautiful skin, although it did not outshine her gorgeous, innocent green eyes. I was really taken by those gems. They gave her an incredible presence, and made it difficult for you to believe that she was such a witty and street-smart person. She had the look of a young girl, but Casey was all woman. At thirty-five years old, she had seen a lot.

I began to think about myself. I was a twenty-two-year-old hotel clerk, who had never left the state of Washington. I worked out when I could three times a week, so I had a decent build; I mean I was a tad under six foot and a bit over 170 pounds. I felt that my body looked good, but I let the ladies speak for me. I didn't have kids, but I had been in a few relationships in my time, so I considered myself an experienced gentleman.

Casey, from what she had explained to me, was a lapsed Catholic, yet that was her religion. She never understood the Catholic way. The deep dark secrets of confession troubled Casey; she wanted to belong to a religion that was open and dealt with the needs of society, and not just the parishioners. Casey's mother Anne, who was an East European Jew, knew about our relationship; she had spoken to me on the phone on several occasions, and she seemed really nice. Anne even sent me a gift as the special someone in her daughter's life: a $200 Timex watch. I treasured it.

Anne had been a victim of the Holocaust at the age of seven. She and her parents somehow managed to escape from Eastern Europe to Italy. Anne spent ten years as a maidservant cleaning toilets. Finally, she made it to the shores of New York in 1950. Anne Worsel, her maiden name, married an American businessman three years after she arrived in Philadelphia. She married for security. According to Casey, Anne never really loved Eugene Balkner, but since he had a fancy last name, she accepted his marriage proposal. Casey was one of three children—her two brothers were younger than her. Casey was apparently being groomed to take over her father's retail clothing business. He had stores in several states along the East Coast; the store closest to Washington was in Chicago. Casey was here to expand the business to the West Coast. That's how I met her, in the Washington Mutual bank branch, while she and I were both doing business there, and we started making small talk.

I liked Casey from the start. Her soft, high-pitched voice, signaling a thoughtful intelligence, instantly piqued my interest. I mean, sure, I'd met a few women who could give me an instant erection, but at my age intellectual stimulation was a higher priority than empty good looks.

Casey's father Eugene really hated me, Casey said. He felt that all Africans—that included African-Americans, of course—were ignorant, barbaric savages who had to be either imprisoned or enslaved. They could not control themselves, especially with women. Although Eugene didn't like me, he still respected his daughter enough to let her run his business.

As I lay in bed thinking, I remembered that Casey had told me her father had ties to some pretty powerful groups. Could it be. . .? The late December chill caught my attention, finally forcing me to shut the window. I looked at my watch; it was 5:30 a.m., which was time to start my day. I went into the hallway and turned the thermostat up to eighty degrees. The boiler instantly came on. The chilly thirty-four degrees outside would keep the motor working until the house warmed up.

Everyone else was still asleep, so I began my morning ritual, 100 military-style pushups and 150 crunches. I didn't want to run today because of the incident earlier this morning. Fifteen minutes later, and perky as the blood raced through my veins, I quickly undressed and hit the shower before my dad began his daily, thirty-minute routine in the bathroom. It was awful when he came out—what could you do? —I was glad to beat him to it this morning.

Everyone began to get up, including my two younger sisters, who both were in their middle teens. They had practically grown up here in my home. Sonya, who was fifteen, and Daisy, all of seventeen, gruffly came into the kitchen. I was the only male my little sisters would let see them like that, their hair matted all over their cute chocolate faces. Grumpy as usual, Sonya went for the cornflakes on top of the refrigerator. As she grabbed the milk, she mumbled, "Morning, Roger."

Pleased, I said, "Love you too, sis."

Daisy, on the other hand, would always hit me up for change. In her eyes, that was a way of showing love. But this morning I saw fear in her eyes, as she looked at me and quickly turned away. I knew instantly that she was aware of what had happened in the early hours of the morning.

I said nothing as Daisy nervously searched for some eggs in the fridge. "Here, let me get that for you, Daisy," I said quickly.

"Thank you, Roger," she replied hoarsely. "I don't know what's wrong with me this morning."

I reassured her, "It's probably puberty, girl!" The three of us shared a quick laugh. After the girls had eaten and gone back to their rooms, Dad finally emerged from his bedroom. He went to check with the girls, asking them if they needed to use the bathroom. They rushed into the bathroom together and locked the door, an odd habit they'd developed. Dad chuckled at the scene. He then excused himself.

"Son, looks like I'll have to use your bathroom."

"Sure, Dad. Just remember to use the spray when you're finished—promise me that."

"You got it, my boy!" Dad quickly excused himself with a few grunts, letting me know he meant business.

Alone again, I reflected on my situation. Ever since my mom, Charlotte, divorced Dad, he and my two sisters had been living with me. I lived in downtown Seattle, which is where I'd been since about the age of nineteen. I was born and raised in Seattle, but my dreams of becoming a doctor were quickly dashed by the harsh conditions of my life as a black person and a poor person. I knew that society held its own dim view of blacks, yet to survive the mean streets, I had to concentrate more on fighting off other blacks than worrying about racism in society.

I delved deeper into my past, wondering whether this would be my last morning together with my family. Would I die today? The question ran through my mind like a distinct possibility. My mother had turned to drugs when I was seventeen. My dad didn't know it, but I was the one who inadvertently introduced Mom to crack. I had been selling crack to make extra money while I was still in high school. Mom found my stash while she was cleaning my room. She confronted me about it, and then she decided that she would hold on to it as a form of punishment. I was thankful that she had not found the $17,000 I had stashed away. That would have probably cost me my life. It was my way of paying off the drug dealer I got the drugs from, a nasty Chinese guy named Won Chu. He was all business. Rumor had it that he killed several of his dealers for shorting him. He was a rather small and weak-looking man, but he could work a knife like a seasoned pro.

Now, while Mom didn't turn me in to the law, for which I was grateful, neither would she give me back the goods. Several months later, Mom went through some personal changes. Dad and my sisters didn't catch on to what was happening, but I did. I was just curious how she had learned to smoke it. I found out when I came home from school early one day and saw a woman that I knew was a crackhead leaving our house. I said to Mom, "Please tell me you're not smoking crack, Mom, please!"

Mom said, "Sit down, son. I have to talk to you." The tears started streaming from my eyes before Mom could say anything else. "You see, Roger, I have cancer and I'm going to have a hysterectomy. I don't want your father to see me this way. So you can tell whoever you want, but I am going to file for a divorce and leave the family."

I sat on the living room couch stunned. I mean we had our share of problems, sure. We lived in a crummy neighborhood and we didn't have much money, but we had each other. That had to count for something.

Mom broke the silence. "Roger, your father already suspects that I'm seeing another man, and he's been nice about it, but believe me, son, he will not be broken up over this. I don't think he has ever really loved me, but he did marry me, so I do give him that much credit."

"But Mom, I thought you and Dad were so happy together."

"Son," Mom laughed, "you have a lot to learn about life." We both laughed at my ignorance and then we hugged each other. Afterwards, I promised Mom I wouldn't say anything to anyone about our conversation. She thanked me and went back to her room. We never again talked about that day. One year later, I bought a home in central Seattle with the money I had saved. Mom vouched for me by saying it was her money. The house needed repair, but it was livable.

About three weeks after I purchased the home, I moved in. I had barely managed to graduate from high school, but I had my own home. I had a job, which I had started while I was a sophomore in high school. I was working at a hotel in downtown Seattle called the Haven. I had started out as a bellhop, which didn't pay much, but my part-time job selling crack helped with my bills.

For a little over a month, I was living in my four-bedroom, two-bath home and making all the necessary repairs. I spent $3,000 fixing up the place. I had $700 to my name by the time I was done sprucing the place up. Making $800 a month wasn't exactly my idea of a dream salary, but I had the opportunity to move up at the hotel.

The biggest surprise came when my parents divorced six months after I moved in. My dad and my two sisters moved in with me. I was taken aback at first, but with the extra financial assistance from Dad, I accepted them into my home. I kept my drug dealing strictly low profile; I didn't want my dad or my sisters to know anything about it. I didn't sell on the streets; I sold during my lunch break downtown. I figured that when I did sell I earned $200 or $300 a day. I didn't sell on weekends, but being a dealer taking a few days off was smart policy. Plus staying small-time kept the law off my back.

I felt the heat of the toaster near my backside, which abruptly brought me out of the reflective state I was in. I came close to having my house torched last night and I needed some answers. I wondered if the men who had been outside my window had left any traces of their visit. I had a breakfast of two bananas, which were a tad overripe, and a slice of toast.

Dad finally came out of my bedroom. "Whew, there is nothing like getting a load off your mind—and your tail, too, for that matter!"

I had to laugh at Dad's humor; the ole boy played life's game like a master. Twenty-two years as a custodian at Boeing, and he earned over $2,000 a month. Plus, he had a 401k. I had to give him credit. My sisters still bathed together at their age and they were singing as they walked out of the bathroom.

"You two are almost fully grown ladies. Why are you still showering together?" I asked playfully.

"Roger, stupid. We don't shower together. We take turns, so just shut up, boy!"

Amused, I let it go. "Alright, divas, have it your way."

"Roger."

"Yes, Dad."

"I need a ride to work, so I'm going with you and the girls. So get ready. I don't want to be late."

"Come on, Dad. You don't have to be at work until ten o'clock. What's the rush?"

"Son, I clock in anytime I want, okay. So just do what I say and hurry up."

"Alright dad."

I've been told that my father and I could pass for twins, yet his deep baritone voice and his salt-and-pepper gray hair set us apart. Dad was as dark as me, maybe even a little darker, but I sometimes wondered where he inherited his dull black color. I certainly felt pride in my heritage, but black is black, and my dad and I were just that. His small but visible potbelly went well with his short afro and long sideburns. Being forty-eight might have slowed most people down, but not my dad. I only wished that he would exercise with me. The older he got, the more he'd feel those joints locking up.

My sisters were finally ready to go to school. Not having a mother to look after them did not slow these two females down. They pulled themselves together like proper young ladies.

I finally called out, "Everybody ready? It's time to get moving."

We all headed outside. My car, a shiny blue, '88 Pontiac Sunbird, was in pretty good shape, in my opinion. Others thought it was in mint condition, but I, ever humble, always viewed my wheels as simply okay.

As we headed toward the detached garage, Daisy screamed. Sonya quickly put her arms around Dad and turned her face away. There, hanging from the old chinaberry tree in the front yard, was a dummy, spray-painted black with a noose around its neck.

"What the hell is that?" Dad whispered. "Who would do this in this neighborhood?" Then he looked at me and muttered under his breath, "It's that damn white woman. Son, why don't you settle down with a nice black woman? We don't need this kind of trouble!"

"Calm down, Dad," I said, feigning calmness myself. "We really can't say who did this. It might be some kids from the neighborhood playing games."

"Well, let's hope so." I could sense that Dad was angry, yet he understood that I was stubborn and wouldn't easily back down. "Well, son, you be careful, you hear? That woman is going to get you planted six feet under, yet."

Upset about the whole thing, I gave Dad my car keys and told him to drop my sisters at school; he could use my car for the rest of the day. Stunned, Dad meekly obeyed. He knew I never loaned my car to anyone, but I had a phone call to make. As Dad and my sisters left home, I got on my cell phone. Casey wasn't home, so I called her shop. "I'm busy right now, Roger, but give me an hour, and I'll call you back."

"Okay, babe. I have some news that won't wait, so call me as soon as you can, love."

"Sure. 'Bye. Love you." As Casey disconnected, I sat at the kitchen table and tried to come up with some answers. Who in hell wanted me out of the way? My engagement to a white woman might be behind it all, but I couldn't be sure. Slavery had ended some time ago, but I still heard rumors of blacks being strung up, so I knew that lynchings were still possible. Yet here in Seattle in 2000? It seemed very unlikely, but, here in my yard, a dummy was strung up in a tree. I went to my room, opened my strongbox, and took out my thirty-eight special revolver. It was old, but I maintained it by oiling it and keeping it from getting damp. I had a box of ammunition, so I loaded it, put it under my pillow, and waited.

Finally, three hours later, Casey called. "Hello, Roger my dumpling, what can I do for you?"

"Look, Casey, I had some trouble last night, and I was curious. What is your dad up to?"

"Well, Roger, strange that you ask. My dad came here late last night, and he's staying at my place. Right now he's out to lunch with some of his friends."

That statement frosted my ass. "Bitch, your old man was here, and you didn't tell me!"

"Now wait a minute, Roger. I wasn't the one who was mad, remember? You're the one who decided not to talk to me, so don't call me bitch."

"Sorry, babe, but something went down last night, and I'm kind of edgy, so don't get too upset with me, okay?"

"Alright, boy, but remember, my dad will be here for another week, and if you want to meet him, just come over to the shop."

"I'll call you, babe cakes, alright? Kiss, kiss."

"Bye, Roger, and be sweet."

"Bye, love."

We both hung up. She called me "boy" to keep me in line. I felt sure that her father had something to do with that little scene outside my room. But for right now I had to call my boss.

Roger

CHAPTER 2

THE HAVEN

It was early afternoon, and the weather was cold and gloomy, when I spoke to my boss. Mr. Gillione was a kind man who thought highly of me. He asked me why I hadn't reported to work today. I told him that I was feeling under the weather. Mr. Gillione suggested that I take a couple of days off and come to work when I was feeling better. I thanked him and wished him a good day.

I didn't miss work much—Mr. Gillione appreciated that. Raymond was his first name, but I always secretly called him Mr. Italian. Mr. Gillione was a short, thin, and balding fifty-year-old with sharp features, hawklike and impressive. He had the looks older women always went ga-ga for. Owning three hotels didn't hurt matters much, either. Yes, I really liked old Gillione, because he respected me. And he always commended me on my good work ethic. "So many young black men throwing their lives away," he would say in his Italian accent. I would always nod in agreement, but deep down I was just like the other drug dealers. I was aware that Mr. Gillione was connected. On more than one occasion I saw him talking to gentlemen who were not your choirboy types. I knew they were mobsters, yet they were always polite, so I never thought twice about how they earned a living.

Mr. Gillione would always tip me well when I ran errands for him while his friends were there. Once I was running an errand for him and I happened to take a close look at one of the sealed envelopes he had asked me to deliver. It had to be cash, about one inch thick and the dimensions of paper money. I didn't want to break the seal, knowing that would be dangerous. So one day soon after that I bought several envelopes of various sizes and hid them in the custodian's room.

I'd always chuckle, thinking back on that. The next time Mr. Gillione gave me an envelope to deliver, I took it, hurried upstairs to the custodian's room, and matched it to one of the envelopes I'd bought. Then I grabbed both envelopes, jumped into the delivery van, and headed out. After driving about a block from the hotel, I tore open the envelope Mr. Gillione had given me. There had to be $5,000 in $100 bills in there. I quickly stuffed the money back into the new envelope and sealed it. After delivering the money, I went back to the hotel and tried to forget about my little indiscretion. Yet thinking about Mr. Gillione always made me smile.

I checked the time; it was four o'clock. Man, the time had really flown by. I looked around my home. Even though it was sparsely furnished with mostly secondhand items, I still was proud the place. The phone finally rang.

"Hello?"

"Hello, Roger sweetheart. What are you up to?"

"I'm waiting to hear some news, girl." I was a little annoyed at Casey, but I didn't let on this time.

"Now look, Roger. I told you my dad was not very fond of you, right?"

"Right."

"Well, I think he's up to something, but that's nothing new. My dad always has a few tricks up his sleeve, if you know what I mean."

"Yeah, babe, I'm beginning to see, especially considering what happened last night."

"Roger, what happened? You didn't say anything before, love."

"Okay, Casey. Somebody was here at my house last night and they left a calling card—a black dummy strung up in a tree."

"Oh, no!" Casey sounded genuinely concerned. "Roger, damn, my dad is serious. It looks like he wants to scare you somehow."

"Well, Casey, I love you. But do you think it's worth it?"

"Roger, I know we are still getting to know each other, but I can't live in fear of my father forever. I have to take a stand."

"Yeah, Casey," I replied, "but I hate being the guinea pig here. I don't want to wind up six feet under just so you can make a point."

"I understand, Roger." Casey then thought about it and finally decided to come clean.

"Hey, Roger, I have a confession to make, but promise me you won't get mad."

"Girl, this is not the time to play games. I'm really skittish about this. Every noise in this house makes me jump."

"Roger, my dad is in some sort of organization, but I'm not exactly sure what it's all about. It's called the European Sheppards and, according to my mom, it's a worldwide organization with a membership of over 5 million. And it's for whites only."

"Damn, Casey, thanks for warning me. I might have walked right into dad's trap if I hadn't known. And, no, I'm not mad at you, okay?"

"Thanks, Roger, I appreciate that. Anyway, my dad wants a pure race, all Aryan blood. That's why he's against anything African, but my mom really likes you, despite Dad."

"Thanks for remembering her, Casey." Right then I kind of wanted to ice the relationship and tell Casey to just forget about me and move on with her life. But I liked her, and I didn't want to give up on her just yet. "Okay, Casey, we have to come up with a plan. Somehow we have to try to talk to your father and see what the problem is."

"Oh no, Roger. That wouldn't work because once he finds out that you'll be with me when we get together, he'll back out of it, and possibly he might even cause real trouble for you and your family."

"Alright. But if you come up with something, call me. I'll be here."

"Okay, Roger honey, I will." We both said our good-byes. I sat in my kitchen, not believing the fix I was in. I had deep feelings for Casey, but I was not in love with her. I was torn; why hang on to her and be killed or badly hurt? Yet I also had my pride, and I wasn't going to turn tail—not now, anyway. I thought about Mom. It had been a while since I had been to see her. I knew she still smoked crack, but she somehow managed to hang on to her home. On certain days I'd give her a fifty. I'd just tell her to hurry up and get off the streets before she got herself arrested. Mom would meekly agree. I hated to see her like that; it broke my heart. She wasn't a zombie—not yet anyway—but give it a few years and things would probably fall apart for her. I'd seen it dozens of times. I ruled out calling her; she might just want another hit. I checked the time—4:37. Just enough time to cook up some shit to sell. But first I cut down that awful dummy from the tree.

Dinner that night was quiet; no one wanted to speak. Dad was tearing through his meal like a madman, while Daisy and Sonya barely touched their food. "Come on girls, eat. You two are worrying me no end. Now, come on, take a bite!" Sonya was the first to speak. "Roger, what's going on with you? I'm scared that someone strung up a dummy in our tree. Man!" I had to reassure the girls and Dad, too. So I decided to try to get them to relax a little. "Okay, everyone, I've prepared this sumptuous meal for us, thinking that it would make us feel less fearful about what happened."

Dad, who was already finishing up his first helping, responded first. "Now look, son, I appreciate the meal. This New Orleans-style gumbo is excellent; the shrimp is very good, too. But, son, we do have a serious problem. Whoever strung up that dummy last night might just come back, and I couldn't bear to see anything happen to my girls."

I had to reassure Dad. "I'm working on things, Dad. Hopefully I can come up with some answers soon, okay?"

Dad, ever cautious but not wanting to alarm my sisters, said, "Alright, son, I'll leave it up to you. I won't say another word until I see you can't handle it. Then I'm going to call the police. I don't care how they feel about Negroes."

"Oh, daddy," Sonya chimed in, apparently feeling that things were under control. Both girls seemed to calm down, and they began digging into their dinners. After finishing eating, I sat down in the living room.

The living room was cozy, with nice beige-white walls. What stood out most was the well-worn turquoise carpet. I should have had it replaced; yet I loved the feel of the thing. Whenever I had visitors, they would express surprise at the color scheme. I, on the other hand, loved the stark contrast of everything. The carpet went well with the used snow-white couch and the matching loveseat. I had bought them at a yard sale close by several years ago for $200—a real steal. I always got things used; it compensated for my lack of legitimate income.

The phone rang, and I took it in my room. It was Chu.

"Hello," I said nonchalantly.

"Hello Roger," Chu said in heavily accented English. "How's my boy?"

"Okay, Chu. What's up?"

"I need to speak to you, tonight, Roger. Can you meet me someplace?"

"Sure Chu. Just tell me where, and I'll be there. You know I'm your main man."

Chu briefly hesitated then said, "Meet me at the Sea Shanty, Roger. See you soon."

Before I could say "'Bye," Chu had already hung up. "Damn, that's one fast-moving dude," I said aloud as I got ready for the trip.

I really liked Seattle in the winter at this time of the evening. Nighttime created something of a bedroom atmosphere. I said good-bye to everyone as I prepared to leave for the evening. "Don't wait up for me, Dad. I'll be gone for a while."

"Okay, son. Be careful now, y'hear?"

It was more of a statement than a question, but I answered anyway. "I will, Dad." Then I hit the night air.

Before I got into my car, I double-checked the yard. Nothing was out of the ordinary. Then it occurred to me that it might be a good idea to get a dog, which would alert me the next time something like what happened last night was going on. However, cleaning up after an animal would be messy. I opened the garage door, got into my car, and headed out. The scenery always caught my attention. I loved the glistening lights of the city, which always overshadowed the glum days of winter.

I was glad that I had taken my heavy jacket along because this was part of the city that I didn't know very well and I might have to do some walking. I remembered that the Shanty was on University Way between 41st and 42nd Streets. Then my automatic memory kicked in near the University of

Washington campus. I usually loved taking in the city as I drove—it gave me a chance to ponder my mission—but tonight I wondered just what Chu wanted. Normally, I met him at the hotel about an hour before Mr. Gillione came in, but tonight, for some reason, he wanted to meet me at the Sea Shanty. I had little trouble finding it, and as tiny as the place was, I could still pick it out easily.

As I entered the restaurant, I saw Chu sitting near the side wall, facing the door. There was not a lot of business at this hour. I quickly glanced at my watch; it was well past 8 p.m. Boy, it took a little longer to get here than I thought it would. I looked around—it was pleasant, and I loved the smell of fried fish, but I wasn't hungry. I went right over to Chu, and before I could say anything Chu stood up and quickly asked me to have a seat.

"What would you like to order, my friend?"

"Well, Chu, I just ate, but I do love breaded shrimp and fries."

"Sure," Chu practically whispered, and then he motioned for the lone waitress in the place to come over. A young Chinese girl, neatly dressed in jeans and a short-sleeve white shirt, buttoned all the way to the neck, she had her long hair tied in a bun. She was thin, but she had a small, pear-shaped figure. She had cinnamon skin that went well with her small, but well-formed head, and was perfect for her doll-like features. "May I have your order, please?" she asked shyly in pretty good English.

"Yes, some breaded shrimp and french fries. And water, please."

"Thank you, sir. It will be ready soon." She left quickly. I checked out her hips as she waltzed away from the table. All the while, Chu was watching me.

"So, Roger, I see you haven't lost your eye for taste," Chu said, letting out a peculiar, high-pitched "Heh, heh." Then he got serious again. "Now, look, Roger, I'm trying to build up business, and I need players who are willing to risk it all with me."

Taken aback, I said to my supplier, "Chu, you know I'm a small-time dealer. Getting too big in this business is dangerous-you know that."

Chu had told me about being locked up in a Chinese prison for eight years, and how he had survived on nothing more than fish and rice. As I eyed him, I could see the raw manhood in him. He was very wiry, with long, thick, jet-black hair. His body build was very compact and muscular. His skin was so dark it was almost ebony, yet the Chinese heritage was unmistakable. Chu was known in drug-dealing circles as someone you didn't mess with.

The young girl returned with my food. "Here you go, sir. Will there be anything else?"

"Just the check, young lady." I tried to sound as professional as I could. She nodded and quickly walked away. Chu continued without the slightest concern for who was listening. "Look Roger, I know your style and that you play it safe, but you're just the man I'm looking for. What do you say?"

"Look, Chu, I hate being part of something I can't control. Man, it scares me to have more than an ounce of shit on me!" The young lady quickly placed the check on the table. I quickly paid her and left a $3 tip.

"Thank you, sir, and come back again," she said.

"I will and thank you, beautiful." She blushed, giggled, and then, peddling backwards, she headed to the kitchen. I enjoyed the moment of flirting.

Chu then dropped the bombshell. "Look, Roger, I want you to come to China with me in a few months. A few guys together with me. You'll be well taken care of, my friend, I promise. What do you say?"

"Chu, damn, I really don't know what to say. I mean my job, my family, you know what about them." Chu was very patient.

"I'll pay you a nice sum, plus, I will front you some shit for a while. How's that?"

Chu was definitely for real. I looked around the small, neat, and well-decorated restaurant. On every wall there were pictures of Asians on medium-sized boats with their hauls of fish. Besides the giant mirrors in the place, the fishermen gave it a Far Eastern appearance. Closing time meant things weren't quite as orderly as at busier moments, but it was obvious that this establishment was a keeper by the way the tables were all covered with the same blue tablecloths and all the wooden chairs matched. I eyed Chu, knowing he meant business.

"Okay, Chu, I'll do it."

The balled fist Chu made let me know he was happy with my decision. He was so happy that he grabbed a couple of my shrimp.

On my way home I listened to the radio—the oldies station. I thought about what I had committed myself to. On the flight to China, I would have a lot of time to think through my decision. The thought of actually going there and no doubt doing something illegal scared me, but I had committed myself.

Once I reached my neighborhood, I drove slowly to see if anything unusual was going on. Nothing seemed amiss, so I drove into the driveway, and got out of my car to open the garage. As I neared the garage, I heard footsteps, and turned around. That's when I felt a sharp pain to the back of my legs. I fell to my knees. At least three times I was hit on the head. Moments later, barely conscious, I didn't feel blood, but it sure stung like hell. Suddenly, I heard three quick shots and, before I crumpled to the ground, I heard footsteps tearing away. The next thing I knew my dad was gently trying to rouse me.

"Son, you okay? Girls!" he yelled out, "call an ambulance."

"No, Dad, I'll be alright. Am I bleeding?"

"No, son, but you do have some pretty good lumps on the back of your head."

Then I muttered, "I knew something went upside my head, but I wasn't sure what it was." Curious, I asked, "Who was it, Dad, and how many were they?"

"It seemed like three or four, son, and they left in a hurry after I let loose a few rounds. I should have aimed for them, but I don't want blood on my hands."

"I understand, Dad. And thanks."

As usual, my dad downplayed it. "I know you'd do the same thing for me, son."

We sat there in silence. Surprisingly, my sisters stayed in their rooms. That was probably for the best; violence never set well with anyone, especially females. As I sat up, I asked, "How long was I out, Dad?"

"To be honest, son, you sort of stumbled into the house and lay on the floor. You weren't out, but you were in a daze. I figured they hit you with a board or something. You're lucky, son."

I knew all too well what my dad meant. A knife or a gun could have inflicted much more damage. "I agree with you, Dad, but it still smarts." As I went to stand up, a searing pain hit me in the back of my legs. Again, I fell to my knees.

"Son, maybe you need a doctor?"

I normally didn't want to get involved with doctors in a situation like this, because the police would usually get involved. Then I reassured Dad, "If it isn't better by morning, I will, I promise." My father grunted his approval and eased back into his room.

I went to my study and got on the computer. I would e-mail Casey and see what she knew about tonight's incident. Whoever it was wanted to either hurt me or scare me away from Casey. Then it hit me: What if what happened was a robbery gone bad? I wasn't sure, but whatever it was, I was definitely going to pack my shit every time I got the chance. After sending the e-mail, I limped into my bedroom. It felt good to be alone. One thing was for sure: The perpetrators now knew that I had someone on my side, and it wouldn't be as easy for them as they originally thought. I lay down on my bed. I silently thanked my dad for his assistance. Despite my pain and lumps, I fell asleep in seconds.

Charlotte

CHAPTER 3

MAMA

I woke up or came to. Whichever it was I knew that I had a splitting headache. My head hurt so badly. It seemed like every time my heart beat, the pain would worsen. I managed to crawl out of bed, and as my mind cleared a little bit, I went for the calendar above my sock drawer. The date was December 18, a week before Christmas. I rarely celebrated, but I would always buy presents for my family. It was the least I could do.

I slowly walked into the study. The room was tidy; one of the girls had probably been here and decided to clean things up. Everything was in place. I turned on the computer. As I waited for it to boot up, I didn't hear any noise in the house. I checked the time; it was 10:30 a.m. Damn! I must have been out while everyone was getting ready for work and school. Finally, I checked my e-mail; Casey had e-mailed me back. "Hello Roger, I thought about what we should plan, and I think you would agree with what I've decided to do. I hired an investigator who is willing to check things out. Hope to hear from you soon. Love, Casey."

Now I realized that Casey was on my side. I didn't bother to return the e-mail. I would call her after I ate something. I could barely get down a piece of toast. For some reason I didn't have an appetite this morning. I called Mr. Gillione and promised to be at work first thing Monday morning. "Good," he said. "I will look forward to your reporting to work, Roger. Get well soon."

"Thanks, Mr. Gillione," I said, trying to sound as sick as possible.

I got off the phone with Mr. Gillione, and quickly called Casey. In an upbeat manner I said, "Hey, girl what's cookin'?"

Casey hesitated, then said, "Look, Roger, I need to talk to you as soon as possible, okay?" Casey sounded worried, so I tried to be reassuring.

"Sure, babe. I'm home alone so you can come over if you want. We can talk over here."

"Great, I'll be over as soon as I can. See you soon, Roger."

"Okay, love." I hung up, pondered what to do next, and decided to call Mom. I dialed the number and waited as the phone rang three times. A groggy voice answered the telephone.

"Hello." She sounded tired.

"Hello, Mother. It's Roger. How are you?"

"I'm fine, Roger. Just a little sleepy. What do you want?"

"Did I catch you in the middle of something, Mom?"

"No, Roger, but I do need a bump."

"Awwh, Mom, I see you're still at it, huh?" I said sympathetically.

This seemed to make her angry. "Well, if a certain person hadn't brought something home, I might not have this problem."

Stung by Mom's words, I tried to regain my composure. "Okay, Mom, I'll bring you some over in a couple of hours. Hold on tight."

This didn't sit well with Mom, who said, "Damn, two hours. Why don't you come over right now?"

"I can't, Mom. But I promise I'll be over as soon I can."

Mom sounded fidgety, but she finally accepted my compromise. "I'll be here, Roger, and don't forget!" Then she abruptly hung up the phone.

I wanted to look presentable for Casey, so I decided to hit the shower. After I showered I felt a lot better. My head was still sore, but I could see straight, and I had regained my balance, so I probably didn't have a concussion. My legs were better, too, but they were a little swollen in the back; still, I was mobile. I dressed in my casual clothes—Levis and a black T-shirt. My house slippers would have to do for now; I didn't feel like putting on shoes.

The doorbell rang. I answered it as quickly as I could; it was Casey. There she stood in a pink, flowery, fluffy dress that came to her knees. Her perfume really got to me. She had her hair straight with no makeup. She didn't have a coat on, so instead of standing there and gawking, I invited her in. As she came in the house, I shut the door.

We embraced, and then we shared a long, well-deserved kiss. I probed Casey's mouth with my tongue. She tasted good, a hint of Crest with a taste of sweet mint. Casey probed back. I could feel myself getting erect. We continued kissing. I began caressing Casey. She felt good to the touch. It felt good to be in her arms. Now I realized how much I loved her. I reached down to her panty line. She was so soft I almost got lightheaded. After the kiss, Casey huskily said, "So, you're here alone, sweetheart."

I was about to explode. I could barely speak. "Come on, lady, let's go to my room. I have something for you." Casey was blushing, which signaled that she was excited. During our previous encounters, she had confided in me that she blushed when she was in the mood. "Am I blushing, Roger?" she asked, her voice coming from deep within her throat.

I said nothing as I led her to my room. Once we shut the door, I lifted up her dress. The pink panties and sexy, low-cut bra sent me over the edge. We both were moaning with anticipation as we undressed each other and raced for the bed. We gave ourselves to each other with absolute abandon. An hour or so later, I felt so refreshed that I had forgotten about my injuries entirely. Casey reminded me of my injury when she rubbed against the back of my head.

"Ouch, girl!"

Alarmed, Casey broke our embrace. "What happened, Roger?"

I knew I couldn't keep it from her now. "Someone jumped me last night and my dad scared them away."

Casey grew hot with anger, and as she sat up in bed, her breasts were exposed. The cute, medium-sized, upturned goodies were so inviting that I had to grab one. This tickled Casey, and her anger subsided a bit. But she managed to say, "I bet my dad had something to do with it."

I tried to be as diplomatic as possible. "Not so fast, Casey. I do have other enemies out there so don't jump to conclusions girl."

Satisfied with my answer, Casey gave in. "Roger, I told you my plans. I hired a private detective who agreed to take the case. He'll start as soon as I give him the go-ahead."

I knew that I was in good hands now. Casey wanted to either help me or warn me about her father. This man seemed dangerous. I had to be careful. Casey and I went over the plans for the private eye. He would get information and then, if he could, he would go to some meetings. The plan seemed foolproof. I knew that a private investigator had to be convincing, or he'd be dead in no time.

We both felt calmer in the afterglow of our intimate encounter. Casey's lovemaking meant a great deal to me. As she was leaving, we briefly kissed and said our good-byes. I watched her drive away and felt that I would be willing to die for her. I dressed without showering. Mom would just have to smell the sex on me.

After I retrieved the cocaine, I drove to south Seattle. I didn't like this part of town. The drug users were rampant, and it was a relatively poor area. The explosion of drugs really decimated parts of this city. It spoiled an otherwise attractive view.

My mother, Charlotte Barns—her maiden name—had been raised in Salt Lake City, Utah. She was one of a handful of blacks to come out of that city. Her family was not rich, but they lived a decent life. Charlotte left home at the age of sixteen to pursue an acting career.

She made it as far as Seattle before she ran out of money. Her parents warned her that if she left home, she shouldn't come back or call them for money. They were Mormons and very strict. Charlotte left Salt Lake to learn how to act, but she wanted to get away from her stepdad as well. He started having eyes for her as soon as she developed some womanly curves. He was white, and he'd convinced Charlotte's mother to become a Mormon. Charlotte hated every minute of it. It was a very restrictive religion, and, to top it off, her stepdad didn't see anything wrong with engaging in sexual relations with her. So Charlotte left her five brothers and sisters to try and make it on her own.

As I pondered my mother's past, I couldn't help but think about how attractive she was. She had naturally red hair with golden skin. Her hair flowed down to her shoulders. At thirty-eight she still had a buxom figure. She had a sweetly expressive face, and her most striking features were her high cheekbones. She was a stunning beauty. Not only could she have become an actress, but she could have been a movie star.

Driving into the driveway, I surveyed the property. This was home—the place where it all began. Yet it was sadly neglected. The yellow stucco had started to fall away in places. It resembled a house that had been abandoned for a couple of years. The lawn seemed to have grown at least two feet high.

As I was reminiscing, I looked up; the deep gray overcast opened up into a torrential downpour. I hurriedly ran to the door and started banging on it. I knocked for what seemed like an eternity. Finally, the door opened. The smell hit me first. It smelled like rotting flesh. Then I noticed how neglected things were. Now dripping wet, I forgot about the rain. Then I saw my mother. She had become painfully thin. Her hair was matted, and she had on an old black nightgown that needed changing. She looked as though she had been in this condition for three or four days.

I tried to sound unfazed by what I was seeing. "Hello, Mom. I'm here."

My mother turned and walked away, mumbling, "Come in, Roger, and have a seat."

I wanted to drop off the crack and leave, but deep down inside, I still loved my mother, and I had to see if she was ready for help. So I said, "Sure, mom." I sat down on the couch. Clothes were strewn everywhere and I couldn't help but notice that Mom hadn't cleaned properly in a few weeks. The couch was the only piece of furniture in the living room. And there was an electric clock on the wall. The paint in the living room was holding its own; it still looked good. The glossy white walls were fairly clean, considering the circumstances.

Slowly, I became accustomed to the smell. "Mom, have you been sick? Can I do something?"

Mom eyed me with a knowing stare that let me know she was still my mother. "Where is it?" she asked and held her hand out. I dug into my pocket and handed her a $50 rock. She grabbed it, and then said gruffly, "Go, and get me something to eat. I'm hungry, okay?" And she hurried into her room.

"No problem, Mom. I'll be right back." Then I checked the weather from the living room window. It was still raining hard. I decided to brave the storm: I would go to the nearest place and buy the cheapest food I could get.

As I was bringing the food back, I couldn't help but admire the cute little cashier at KFC. She winked at me and smiled, then said flirtatiously, "Have a nice day, handsome." I was so thrilled, that I forgot all about the rain. I sang all the way back to Mom's house. The door was ajar, so I walked in. Mom had straightened up a little. She had more pep in her step now.

"Here's the food, Mom. I know how you like chicken." I handed her the food, which she seized as if she hadn't eaten in weeks.

Without hesitating, she began wolfing down the food. I hadn't picked up a drink for her, feeling that I had done enough by purchasing the food. Mom didn't seem to mind. She was busy eating. In between bites and spitting out just a little bit of her chicken, Mom said, "Clean up the house for me, Roger. I don't feel good today." I understood Mom, so I agreed to do it.

It took me two hours, but I cleaned the kitchen, the bathroom, and the dining room. I used most of the Pine Sol and Comet; I was surprised that Mom still had any left. The house now had the fresh smell of pine.

The bathroom was filthy. I couldn't believe Mom would let herself go like that, but in the crack business I learned to expect anything. Yet, I was curious about the dried vomit in the bathroom—it made me sick just thinking about it. I wondered what Mom was doing to make herself so ill. Maybe she was drinking a little too much. Anyway, I wanted to get to the bottom of this. After I put away the last of the dishes and the few pieces of silverware in the house, I went into the living room and sat down next to Mom on the couch.

Mom had finished the five-piece meal and the empty bag lay on the floor with the chicken bones on top of it. The biscuits were untouched. Mom was in a state of semiconsciousness. Concerned, I asked, "What's wrong, Mom?"

Mom came to and looked at me. She seemed distant, and then she finally spoke to me. "It's not the same, Roger. It's not the same!"

I grabbed Mom by the shoulders and sternly asked, "What's not the same Mom?"

As she tried to look at me, Mom began to cry and blurted out, "I'm on heroin, son, and I feel awful about it!"

"When did you get started on that shit, Mom?" I was shocked. Crack was bad enough, but the big H! No one was fool enough to mess with that. I tried to sound reassuring. "When did you start, Mom? Maybe you can stop before you get hooked."

Mom looked at me with a hopeless stare and cried out, "Six months ago! I knew it was the wrong thing to do, but I never dreamed I would get this sick!"

Stunned, I just sat there on the couch. I smoked weed once in a blue moon, but I needed something now to soothe my nerves. We sat on the couch in silence for about an hour. Finally, I got up the nerve to say, "Do you have anymore crack, Mom? I need a hit."

Mom looked at me with a devilish grin, and she laughed slightly before she said, "When did you start, Roger?"

"A little while ago, Mom. I do it every now and then. Get me some!" I had to make up a quick lie to convince Mom to hand some over.

Mom went into her room and moments later came back out, holding a glass pipe with about a $5 hit on it. "Damn, Mom," but I took it anyway. She gave me a cotton swab on a wire, then she lit it.

She said, "This is alcohol. It won't hurt," I tried my best to act like an experienced smoker, so I went on instinct. I put the fire on the rock and inhaled. I could see the smoke coming through the pipe. Mom yelled, "Hit it hard, Roger!" And I did. At that instant my world was transformed. It was an instant high. I felt so good that I wondered why I hadn't tried this before. I began to dance around Mom's home, feeling as if I weighed no more than a feather. Then I began singing, "Just a Touch of Love," by the group Slave. Halfway through the song, my euphoria changed. I started feeling so low that I wanted to cry. I sat down and tried to roll myself into a ball. Mom noticed this change and commented, "Roger, you have to keep hitting the pipe to stay up."

I knew that getting hooked on crack was the last thing I needed. So I refused. "No, Mom, I don't need any more of that shit. I'm not going out like that!" I could see it all going up in smoke and I couldn't let that happen.

"I wish I was as strong as you, Roger. I hate myself." Mom began to cry long and hard. She had been holding this in—I could tell—so I let her have her cry. I went into the kitchen and looked in the refrigerator. There was half a bottle of Mad Dog. I grabbed it and took a swig. Damn, rotgut sure could break a man down. I took two more strong swigs, put the bottle back in the fridge, and then sat down at the kitchen table and waited.

Mom finally came into the kitchen. "Look at me, a grown-ass woman crying like that, and in front of my son of all people." The Mad Dog began to talk to me; it had me pretty relaxed. I had recovered from the crack, but I had a bad taste in my mouth. I wanted to help Mom, so I suggested that she check herself into a rehabilitation center in another state. "That would be great, Roger, but where would I get the money, huh?"

"Why not sell this house?" I knew several people who would buy Mom's house as is, and that would get her on her feet. "Let me look into it, Mom, and I'll get back to you, alright?" Mom seemed to have a new light in her eyes. She looked into my eyes and said, "Roger, I'm going cold turkey. When we sell this place I'm going to rehab, I promise.

I knew my mother, and I felt that she would give it her best shot. I looked at her. She was still attractive, but you could tell that she was hooked on drugs by her appearance and the fidgety way she moved. She rambled at times, too. Her weight was the giveaway: She was, as they say, "dope thin."

Then Mom began giggling like a schoolgirl, a laugh that turned hysterical. "What is it Mom?" I wanted to get in on the fun.

"Well, Roger," she said, finally regaining her composure. "You remember I told you that I had a hysterectomy for cancer? Well, I didn't. I never had cancer, and I still have my reproductive organs."

I was shocked, but I had my doubts. "So why did you leave Dad?"

Mom looked me straight in the eye and replied, "I was ashamed of myself for being on drugs, Roger. And I knew your father would never accept that."

I felt awful, knowing that Mom had started using because of me. "Mom, I know you must hate me deep down inside, but I never expected you to find my stash and then use it! I never would have guessed." I began to cry silently. I had broken up my parents' marriage over my drug dealing, but I felt worse that my mother was in this condition.

Mom felt my pain and came over and embraced me. We must have held each other for some time, both shuddering with tears.

That night at home I contemplated my situation. I called several people, and Leon, an underground investor, promised to give Mom $60,000 upfront for the house, but she would have to leave immediately. I agreed on the spot. Leon and I would meet in front of my mother's in a couple of weeks. With that transaction completed, I thought about my experience with crack. Damn, if I had to use all my power to resist the stuff, I'd never try it again. I also thought about my trip to China. I was hoping Chu would call it off, but I knew from experience that he wouldn't. I would apply for a passport this week.

"Roger, dinner's ready. Come and eat!" Daisy yelled through the door.

I snapped out of my deep thoughts. "I'll be right there," I yelled. I checked my revolver; it was still tucked under my pillow. Then I went and joined my family for dinner.

My two younger sisters were still children as far as I was concerned, but they had actually become mature young ladies. Sonya was the younger and the larger of the two. She also had a masculine aura about her. Still, she was undeniably attractive. Sonya carried herself like a lady, but around other females she liked to be the one in control. Most people said she resembled my father and me. Daisy, on the other hand, looked a lot like Mom. She even had Mom's natural red hair. Her figure could have been Mom's in earlier years.

I sat down to eat, and the meal looked great. Baked pork chops with cabbage and fried green tomatoes. I really loved fried tomatoes. After we said grace and began eating, I noticed that Dad was in a fair mood. Not good, but fair. So I decided to needle him. "How's work going, Dad? Okay?"

Dad hesitated just a little then said. "It went like a day at work. son. A lot of cleaning and watching passenger jets." From his answer I surmised that it would be okay to mention Mom.

"I went to see Mom today, and we had a good talk."

Dad stiffened and looked at my sisters. He knew they loved their mother dearly, so he tried to sound respectful. "Now, son, you know that your mother isn't speaking to me. I haven't spoken to your mother in some time."

Pleased, I wanted to push the issue. "Well, Dad, Mom decided that she would go into rehab today, and she and I are working on a plan."

Dad stopped eating, looked at me hard, and yelled, "Why didn't you tell me your mother was on drugs? Son, I trusted you . . ." He got up and stormed away from the dinner table.

I was hurt, but I had to tell him. Daisy picked up a TV tray, while Sonya took the dinner plate and the silverware and they both went into Dad's room.

When they came out of Dad's room, Daisy spoke first. "He's crying, Roger. Maybe you can talk to him when he's feeling better."

Sonya seemed teary-eyed before asking, "Does Mom still work, Roger?"

"I'm not sure, sis, but Mom will need our support. I kind of miss having her around, y'know." Both girls silently agreed with me. We all sat down and began eating again. I settled down, thinking this would be a long night.

Roger

CHAPTER 4

THE PRIVATE DICK

A week had passed since we last mentioned Mom. My sisters were on Christmas break and they spent a lot of time cleaning the house and chattering among themselves. Casey and I had spoken several times over the last week. The private investigator had found out plenty. Allen Wilson, all of twenty-seven, had been a private detective for five years. He ran his own company and by the looks of things was pretty thorough. Tall and slender, Allen was a cut above your typical PI. His handsome yet rugged features went well with his dark brown hair, but his most compelling feature was his deep baritone voice. No doubt, he had his among the ladies. I even noticed Casey eyeing him when we had our first meeting, but I couldn't let jealousy get in the way—at least not now.

Allen had found out where the Sheppards' meetings were held. It was a little hole in the wall near Elliot Street by the bay. The PI had posed as a drifter who wanted some change, and he was welcomed warmly by the Sheppards. According to Allen, the group was well organized, but most of the men were upper-class guys who brought in local lower-class thugs as muscle. Allen thought these were probably the ones who had targeted Roger Singleton, a man whose name was well known in the Sheppards' circle, courtesy of Eugene Balkner. Eugene had boasted that he wanted a piece of Roger. Allen also found out that the group was akin to the KKK and held feelings of Aryan superiority. For now, Allen was playing it cool.

Once Allen gave Casey this information, she told me. Now I was sure of it—Eugene Balkner definitely had it in for me.

I had just finished loading some supplies in the supply closet when Mr. Gillione called me over. "Roger, I want to give you a little Christmas bonus." He then winked at me and handed me an envelope.

"Thank you, Mr. Gillione. I really appreciate it!" Mr. Gillione was all smiles as he shook my hand.

"You have been a loyal employee, Roger, and I want to thank you for working here." Mr. Gillione smiled and hurried back to his office.

Madeline Thompson, my assistant, came over. "What was that all about, Roger?" Always one to be nosy, Madeline caught everything, but usually said nothing.

I replied, "Oh, a little Christmas love, girl." I gave her a light pat on the back, adding, "Didn't you get a gift from Mr. Gillione?"

She blushed and said, "I sure did, but I was curious what you two were up to." Everyone in the hotel knew Madeline was Mr. Gillione's plaything, but no one seemed to mind. It was the way things went around here. Madeline wasn't beautiful, but she was good-looking in her own way. A shapely woman with free-flowing brown hair, Madeline had an upturned nose and a chubby face. She had soft facial features that appealed to men. At nineteen, she had few professional skills, but her feminine charms—and Mr. Gillione's lust— kept her employed.

Since business was slow today, I decided to take an early lunch. I had about $200 worth of crack in my car, so I headed downtown. My customers knew me, and as soon as they spotted me they began to come out. It wasn't raining today, but the sky was overcast—graying and dark. The addicts were business people and working-class folks who loved the white lady, cocaine. I would sell to five or six people then go somewhere else. I'd wait ten to fifteen minutes and begin selling again. The usual crowd of people shuffling through didn't pay much attention to what was going on. I liked that.

I sold $150 worth of crack and decided to call it a day. As I was going back to the hotel, I spotted Chu.

"Hey, Roger!" he yelled. I stopped and waited for Chu, then I reprimanded him.

"Don't call my name like that, man. It's bad for business."

Chu quickly understood, so he replied sarcastically, "Well, excuse me, sir." He was wearing lively black tights with heavy-duty boots. I patted him on the back and we begin walking, Chu broke the uneasy silence, "Look, Roger. I want to know: Do you still plan on going to China with me?"

This was my chance to back out, but I knew that Chu would not forget it, nor would he ever forgive me. "You know I'm ready, Chu. So what brings you here?"

Always brazen, Chu whipped out an ounce of powdered cocaine. "Here, Roger, a gift from me, my man."

I grabbed the ounce and quickly put it in the pocket of my goose-down jacket. "Thanks, Chu, I'm almost out anyway."

Without another word, Chu turned and walked away. I was used to his antics by now, so this didn't surprise me. I headed back to the hotel and prepared for work the rest of the day.

At home that night I counted the bonus Mr. Gillione had given me. A total of $300—wow! This was great. Now I had extra money for Christmas gifts. I knew that giving my little sisters $100 apiece would make them happy, but as far as Mom and Dad, I would have to get them each a special card, as I always did. Tonight Daisy's boyfriend, Pal Simmons, was over. He and Daisy were still in the puppy-love stage of their relationship. Pal was a bespeckled young man with mild acne and a bit of a paunch. He wore his hair in a small afro, yet he reminded me of a mulatto. This kid was an intellectual in the making. I think that was the reason Daisy fell for him. They both were seventeen and students at Garfield High School. Both were math whizzes, currently studying calculus. I was proud of my little sister. Sonya, on the other hand, was content with general studies. Tonight, Daisy and Pal were going out to the Garfield Bulldogs' basketball game. Not my idea of a night on the town, but I didn't mind Daisy going as long as she invited Sonya to accompany them. As they left, I wished them a fine evening. Dad had called earlier and told me he'd be working late. I really didn't want to grill Pal. Besides, he seemed like such a decent boy. Furthermore, that was Dad's responsibility.

I decided to cook up the ounce Chu had given me. I had it ready in twenty minutes, so afterwards I called Mom. "Hello, Mom. It's Roger. How are you?"

Mom seemed ecstatic. "Hey, Roger, guess what? I haven't had any drugs since we've talked. The first three days I was shaking and vomiting pretty bad, but now I'm feeling a little better."

I had to know, so I said, "Have you really been using for six months, Mom?"

I felt Mom hesitate, and then she said, "I think it's actually about four months. I don't know why I started, Roger, but I'm sorry I did. That stuff kind of ruined me, you know."

Since we were talking, I asked Mom again, "Are you still working?"

"Well, Roger, I saved $50,000 from my job as a beautician, and I worked on and off for several years, but the past year I've been living off my savings."

I had to admire Mom's savvy. The ole girl really had learned a lot about survival over the years. Then I changed the subject to her property. In another week Mom would have to leave her home to go into rehab. "Mom, are you still ready for treatment in a couple of weeks?"

"Roger, I've been praying for the day when I could start over and really do something with my life," she said, excitement rising in her voice.

"I'm so glad to hear that, Mom. I'll get in touch with Leon, and see what we can do about getting that deal done, okay?" Mom had really impressed me by staying clean over the last week or so.

"Okay, Roger, you do that and stay in touch. Love you." Then Mom quickly hung up.

I had voice mail, so I checked it. Casey had left a message.

"Roger, meet me at the hotel where you work tonight at twelve o'clock. we have to talk. See you then." As I hung up the phone, I wondered what Casey wanted to discuss with me at that time of night.

The meeting was going just as planned. Eugene Balkner, a guest from Philadelphia, wanted to address his fellow brethren from Seattle before he headed back home. "Gentlemen, I came to this great city to visit my fellow Sheppards. Now we all have the same agenda, men." Balkner sized up the audience of about twenty-five men and went on. "We can't force the government to send away the darkies, the spics, waps, or any of these other mud people who are destroying our beautiful country!" Balkner looked around the small room. He knew he had these men's respect, so he added with force, "Now, as if it isn't enough that we let them in our great land—America—now they want our women!" The group began voicing their support by saying, "Screw niggers like they're screwing our women and let's keep the spics in the cotton fields!" The men begin giving each other handshakes and hugs.

Balkner, sensing his complete control over the crowd, ended the meeting with a final statement. "Gentlemen, our fine God will not let these heathens corrupt us completely. If we have to, men, we will take our women back, even if we have to kill for them!"

This was all Allen Wilson needed to hear. When the meeting was over and the men were standing around drinking coffee, Allen pretended he had to take care of some business elsewhere. As he headed for the door, Balkner came over to him.

"What's the rush, Wilson? I thought you might want to have some hot coffee before you get out into the chilly night."

Allen knew he had to strike a racist note, so he said, "Sir, I don't want those hoodlums out there taking my belongings."

Balkner seemed to relax a little before he said, "I get your point, young man."

Wilson sized Balkner up. A tall man, as tall as Wilson, but much broader, Balkner looked like he was in excellent health and he carried his weight well. Wilson knew that Balkner had worked his way up the ladder. Balkner's coarse hands and the permanent sun-scorched skin impressed Allen. Balkner was well-groomed, but not very handsome—he had extremely large ears, which stuck out from his head, and a large, bulbous nose. The squinty eyes were rather prominent on his rather large, round head. Wilson also noticed that Balkner dressed well and had a booming voice. "Well, great meeting you, Mr. Balkner."

Before Allen could leave, Balkner gently reached for him and said, "Son, I don't know much about you, but you'd make a fine Sheppard. Now, of course, there are other things you need to do before joining."

Allen Wilson was wary of what was coming next. He had to play it cool. "Well, Mr. Balkner, we'll talk again, hopefully before you leave Seattle."

Balkner, not to be outdone, gave Allen his business card. "Call me, son. We definitely have to talk."

Allen took the business card. "Sure, Mr. Balkner. I'll call you sometime. Now, excuse me, I've got to run." Allen walked out, waving as he left the meeting.

I met Casey at the hotel. "Hey, Roger, I'm glad you made it." Casey was dressed in a blue pantsuit. She wore a heavy dark-blue raincoat. As I dug in my pocket and retrieved my hotel room key, Casey squeezed my butt, and I said, "That feels good, girl. Do it again."

"I don't want to start something I can't finish, Roger. Plus, I don't have much time."

We went into the hotel and I led Casey up to room 31. Michael, the night clerk, watched us walk by without a second thought. Mr. Gillione had given me a room to myself as long as I worked for him. Casey didn't take off her coat, which signaled that she didn't want to fool around.

"Look, Roger, my dad really means business. Allen went to a meeting tonight and Dad wants to talk to him." Casey gave me a frightened look.

I wanted to reassure her, but she knew her father better than I did, so I offered a suggestion. "Casey, why don't we walk right into the lion's den?" I was looking out for my family as well. I didn't want to draw them into this dangerous situation if I could help it.

"What do you mean, Roger?"

"You and I should move in together. That would make the Sheppards think twice about trying to harm me."

Casey seemed surprised, and then she got a certain gleam in her eyes. "You know, that would be a great idea, Roger. When do you want to move in?"

I thought about it, and figured it would be better for me to live with Casey than for her to live at my place. "Give me a few days, Casey. I have to talk to my dad and straighten some things out, okay?"

Casey reassured me that she would be waiting. We left the hotel and went our separate ways, but not before a quick but passionate kiss.

Arriving home, I noticed that the front door was open a crack, and as I pulled into the driveway, Dad opened the door and looked out. It gave me great comfort knowing that my dad had my back. I eased the car into the garage and met Dad at the front door.

"Thanks, Dad. I mean it." I was really proud of how well my dad cared for the family. As we went inside, I remembered telling Dad about Mom earlier, so I started the small talk first. "How are the girls, Dad? Did they make it home alright?"

Dad gave me a knowing pat on the back. "Son, you know Pal Simmons is a good man. He brought the girls home by 12:30. He even wanted to stay here with them."

We both laughed at Pal's clumsy stab at romance.

"Dad, you don't think Pal was trying to. . ."

"I don't know—maybe. My girls are becoming attractive young women, son. I can't keep them babies forever."

I admired Dad's ability to let his children grow up. "Dad, I'm sorry about Mom, but I had to let you know."

He seemed like he was ready to talk about it now. "Son, tell me something. How long have you known this?"

I was too ashamed to tell Dad the whole truth, so I told him only enough to satisfy his curiosity. "I've known for sometime, Dad, but I knew it would hurt you. I know how you feel about Mom."

Dad nodded and said, "I figured when she wanted to leave me that it was more than another man. Roger, did you know that when your mother worked I let her to save all her money?"

Dad wanted to get some things off his chest, so I ran with it. "No, I didn't, Dad."

We looked at each other and touched hands before he continued. "She was a firecracker, son, but I knew how to keep her ass still. You've got to give it to them good, son, or they'll walk away from you."

I knew a little about women, but Dad's theory seemed to make a lot of sense. Impressed, I wanted to dig a little deeper. "So, Dad, when did the sex stop?"

"It didn't, but I wasn't able to do it like I did when I was younger. Charlotte understood, she didn't complain, but I knew she'd satisfy herself at times. It didn't bother me though."

I laughed a little before I said, "Damn, Dad, I didn't know you had it in you. . ." This was moment to go further. "Dad, I'm planning to move out shortly. I wanted to let you know first."

He looked up to the ceiling, avoiding eye contact, before he said, "I understand that you're a man, son, so I won't hold you back. But does this trouble you're having have anything to do with it?"

Tears welled up in my father's eyes. I'd known him all my life, and he was always there for me. It would be hard on me, but I had to do it. I didn't want to tell Dad that I was trying to protect him and the girls—he wouldn't have it. I answered Dad's question. "I'm leaving because I want a chance to learn about my fiancée, and besides, it's time for me to move on." Dad wouldn't cry, but his tears were on the brink of falling. He didn't comment on my decision, even though he frowned on my relationship with Casey.

I woke up Saturday morning with a load off my mind. I decided to leave all my possessions here and take only my clothes and my revolver with me to Casey's. She had an apartment near Lakeside Avenue in upscale Seattle. I had never been to her condo, but from Casey's stories, I knew it had to be nice. I exercised, showered, and went into the kitchen. I ate a couple of pieces of fruit and turned on the oldies station. I looked around my modest abode. It would be tough leaving, but this would benefit Dad and my two sisters. I refused to live in fear. Initially, I planned to wait for my sisters to come into the kitchen, but I decided to go into their room instead. Both girls sat up quickly when I entered. I said, "Morning," and handed each girl a $100 bill. Both of them thanked me profusely. I hugged them both and wished them a Merry Christmas.

Leon wanted to meet me over at my mother's home. I arrived before him and knocked on the door. Mom answered and, all things considered, she looked good. This time I managed to give her a kiss on the cheek.

"Thanks, Roger, why don't you come in?"

I stepped inside, and noticed that the place was straightened up. I didn't pick up that awful odor; it smelled of disinfectant. Mom even had the grass in the front yard mowed. "I see you have been busy, Mom."

"Yes, Roger, I decided to go to Utah after I complete the program. I might just look up my family. Maybe even try to locate my dad."

I was impressed with Mom's clear, rational thinking. Before I could answer, there was a knock on the door; it was Leon. "Come in Leo, how's everything?"

"Just fine, young man." Leon quickly eyed Mom and me before saying, "Who am I doing business with?"

Mom's silence allowed me to speak up. "With me, of course."

Leon then said, "Do you mind if a couple of my people look the place over?"

"No, not at all."

Leon opened the door and motioned with his left hand. Moments later three middle-aged black men—apparently Leon's inspectors-strode into Mom's home. Startled, she yelled, "Let me get my purse first." When mom came back with her purse, the three men began thoroughly checking out Mom's place.

It took them roughly thirty minutes. Leon checked out the grounds. Finally, the inspectors all congregated outside, while we prepared to do our business inside.

Leon came back into the house and gave me a quizzical look before saying, "I can give you $55,000." His matter-of-fact tone startled me; I wanted to hold out for more, but I knew I had to get Mom into rehab before she changed her mind.

Mom broke the silence. "It sounds good to me. What about you, Roger?"

"Well how soon could we get the money, Leon?"

"I can write you a check right now, but then I would give you twenty-four hours to leave the premises."

Curious, I asked, "Why such short notice?"

Leon paused and said curtly, "If I'm going to turn any profit, the quicker you leave, the better. Now let me see the deed."

I knew Leon was an underhanded businessman, but I had to respect his bluntness. "Okay, Leon, we'll take it."

Leon was presumptuous: He had already written out a check—all he had to do was sign it over. I said nothing as he gave me the check.

"Good day, folks," Leon said as he left. I watched him head out. A lean man, Leon stood about 5 foot 7. He was a very dark-complexioned man. He wore a goatee and had a shaved head. He looked like the athlete who never quite made it to the big time. His cigar smoke still lingering in the air, I wondered how Leon made his money. Drugs, money laundering, or was he coming by it honestly? I really didn't care, but I would be upset if this thing didn't go off well. I knew I had Chu covering my back, but even then, how far would Chu go? I was on my own.

Mom had packed two suitcases and an overnight bag. "Roger, I don't need the little furniture that's left, and besides, I already sold everything that was worth anything."

I knew Mom wasn't stupid, but I still had to ask. "Do you have any money?"

She smiled, looked at me, and said, "I have some money, Roger—over $20,000. I spent a lot of my savings, but I do have some left."

I knew Mom wouldn't give away anything valuable; she was too shrewd to do that. "Okay, let's go, Mom."

We took one last look at what used to be the family home and then we walked out. Since tomorrow was Christmas, I decided to bring Mom home with me.

As we walked in, Mom started trembling. She said, "Roger, I have not seen my girls and your father for years. I don't know what to say!" I reassured her, and we went into the living room. Daisy and Sonya were busy fussing over the small Christmas tree in the center of the living room. They caught sight of their mother, dropped what they were doing, ran to her, and gave her a big bear hug. They stood there, laughing, crying, and kissing for some time.

Dad came out of his room at that point. "What's all the . . . Charlotte! Girl, I missed you!" Dad exclaimed. My sisters stood back and watched as Mom and Dad approached each other. "Merry Christmas, Theo," Mom said.

"Merry Christmas, babe." Dad was one smooth operator.

"What are we eating for Christmas everyone?" Mom asked shyly. She was back in her role as the mother again. For that I was truly grateful.

Roger

CHAPTER 5

DEATH THREAT

The family enjoyed Christmas like never before. Mom and Dad, of course, were getting to know each other again. I was even hoping that they would get back together, but I knew that was wishful thinking. Both of them knew that the pain of their breakup was too great to overcome so quickly.

I had put off moving in with Casey until after Christmas. Let everyone get reacquainted, and then we would decide what we would do from there as a family. I hadn't had any problems with Casey's father recently, and that made me uneasy. When things were going well, that's when you had to worry.

I had spoken to Casey on Christmas Eve. She told me that her father had gone back to Philadelphia and that she too would be going back for a few days. She told me that she was leaving a key for me under the doormat. Risky, I thought. But maybe it was a little old-fashioned cleverness that might fool would-be thieves. I didn't talk to Allen Wilson directly: I didn't want to blow his cover. But Casey had told me plenty.

Eugene Balkner wasn't one to play games. He liked Allen Wilson. The young man had made a good impression on him. After the last meeting, Eugene decided to call his young protégé. Eugene loved the contrast between Philadelphia and Seattle. The lush greenery and mountains of Washington State seemed like a paradise to him. Philadelphia was a manmade haven, where only the wealthy prospered. Eugene knew many good people who fell victim to poverty trying to make it in the so-called "City of Brotherly Love." A frugal man, Eugene lived in a relatively low-class part of that city, not too far from Veterans' Stadium, near 21st Street.

Eugene never liked mixing with other races, but he knew that being labeled a racist was bad for business. He also liked the money minorities spent at his establishments.

He fumbled in his wallet for Allen Wilson's phone number. When he found it, he went into the rest room and shut the door. Eugene dialed the long-distance number. Trying to sound casual, he said, "Hello, Allen? How are you? This is Eugene Balkner. I wanted to talk to you."

"Hi, Mr. Balkner. Good to hear from you."

"Now you know that I can't be in Seattle and Philadelphia at the same time, so I want to ask you to do me a favor. I want you to take care of something for me." Eugene was careful not to mention precisely what he wanted. "I have a little problem with things in Seattle, and I'll write you a letter and let you know what I want you to do. I'll be in touch." Then he abruptly hung up.

Eugene didn't know Wilson, and, according to the members in Seattle, it was odd for a new person to just happen to walk in during meetings. Normally, a new person got in touch with an established member. Wilson had just walked in unannounced. Eugene was no fool; he wanted Wilson to prove that he was legit. Eugene would usually let local toughs handle Roger Singleton. But to find out if Allen Wilson were an undercover agent or not, Balkner would write Wilson a letter instructing him to kill Roger Singleton. Eugene wanted to be sure that no one could find out what he was up to; if they did, he'd be ruined. After writing the letter, Eugene put it in an envelope, stamped it, and drove it to the post office to mail it.

Right now Casey wasn't even sure who her father was. She had always known that he didn't like people who weren't white, but to go as far as to tell her who she could and could not date was just ridiculous. Casey had a rebellious streak, but despite that she felt that her father had her best interests at heart. However, he was taking things too far this time. A knock on the door snapped Casey out of her thoughts. It was her dad.

"Casey, come out into the dining room. It's time we had a little chat."

It would be hard for Casey to act as though nothing had happened, but she had to at this point. She finally came out of her room, which was just as she had left it when she moved to Seattle almost two years ago—her mother insisted on it. Casey appreciated her mother's thoughtfulness, but she wished her mother had more of a backbone. Her room was small, but well decorated. The stuffed teddy bears filled one corner. The light-blue walls contrasted with the light-brown rug, but Casey liked it because it had been there for as long as she could remember. Her single bed seemed to be too small for her now, but she still liked sleeping in it.

"Yes, Dad?" Casey said groggily, as she feigned that she had been sleeping.

"Come on, Casey, and have a sit-down next to Dad."

Casey reluctantly went over and sat down next to her dad.

Eugene put his arm around his daughter. Casey didn't flinch. "Casey," he said, as he looked intently at his daughter, "I don't want you to go back to Seattle. I'm willing to sell the business and have you run all the businesses on the East Coast for me."

Casey was surprised at her dad's proposal. She liked his offer, but she knew why he was making it. She tried to pretend she didn't know the reason. "Gee, that sounds good, Dad, but I've kind of grown to like Seattle."

This didn't sit well with Eugene, who replied, "Well, sweetheart, I've already put the business on the block, and there's been an offer—a pretty good one, too. What do you say, Casey?"

In her heart Casey began to despise her dad. "I really like Seattle, Dad. And besides, Philadelphia gets on my nerves. I don't think I could live here and be happy anymore."

Eugene stormed out of the room, but not before yelling, "Dammit, young lady, don't make things difficult. Just do what I say!"

Casey didn't want to push it with her father. She knew he could be violent, so she just sat there until he left.

After Eugene was gone, Casey got on the phone. She had looked up the telephone number of the bank she dealt with—the Washington Mutual branch in Seattle. "Hello, may I speak to Don Larson?"

"Hold, please." Casey listened nervously to the customary background music for over five minutes before a well-rehearsed voice came on the line. "Don Larson speaking. How can I help you?"

Casey was getting antsy. "Hello, Mr. Larson. This is Casey Balkner, of Balkner Retail, and I wanted to make a transaction." She bit her fingernails as she spoke. "I want to put $200,000 into my personal account from the Balkner retail business account."

Larson cleared his throat, took down Casey's account numbers, and said, "Let me take care of that for you, Miss. Balkner." Moments later he came back on the line. "Okay, Miss Balkner. This will leave your retail account with a balance of $50,000. Anything else I can do for you?"

Casey liked Larson's smooth alto voice. "No, Mr. Larson, that's all."

"Have a good day, Miss Balkner."

Casey loved how he hung onto the words as he spoke. "Thanks, Mr. Larson, and you, too." Casey hung up and went to the kitchen to make herself a sandwich.

The family went to Casey's brother's place for Christmas. Hal Balkner had turned twenty-five two months ago, and he'd just been released from the National Guard. He'd served in the Guard for six years. He was a security guard by trade. Hal wasn't very bright—Eugene even suggested that he was a bit retarded—but Casey had adjusted to her little brother. William, the youngest at twenty-two, couldn't make it. He was doing time for assaulting a Japanese man in New Jersey over a seat on the bus. Eugene had practically disowned his younger son, vowing never to see him in prison. Nevertheless, Eugene still sent his son money every month while William did his time.

Hal's fiancée Deborah was a fine woman, according to Eugene. She was the perfect housewife, who loved to serve the needs of her man. Casey grew tired of her father patronizing Hal. He would say things like, "Son, you've really made me proud" or "I wish all of my children could make rational decisions like you, son."

Casey knew her father was directing the comments at her, but she smiled and chimed in. "Yeah, Hal, you've really done well for yourself." Deep down inside, however, Casey felt sick. First of all, Hal lived in the poor section of South Philadelphia. To top it off, Hal's apartment was infested with bugs and rodents. Casey tried to hide her disappointment as best she could, and it seemed to work because no one noticed. Casey respected Hal, but she was perturbed that he wouldn't join the family business. Hal didn't have the confidence to handle large amounts of money, so he decided to do something else, and became a security guard at Veterans' Stadium. This didn't sit well with Casey; still, she felt she had to show him a certain measure of respect.

After eating and visiting for several hours, Eugene, speaking for the family, decided it was time to leave. As they were leaving, Casey sized up the seemingly happy couple. Hal, who looked a lot like his father, stood a bit over 6 feet tall. His muscular physique made up for an otherwise downright ugly appearance. Casey loved her brother well enough, yet he had an uncanny resemblance to her father—the big ears, the large nose and that big round head. Casey was grateful that she got her looks from her mother.

Deborah Montgomery, Hal's fiancée, was pure trailer-park trash. She and Hal met while on their two-week assignment in the National Guard two years ago. They were both tall, Deborah a little bit shorter. She was fairly attractive, with blue, almond-shaped eyes and a square jawline. Her long brown hair fell to her shoulders. Her nose was thin, long, and pointed, yet she had a pretty smile. But what really gave Casey the impression of trailer-park trash was the way Deborah spoke. Boy! She must have been straight out of Arkansas or Alabama. Deborah talked as though she had little or no education. The "you all's" and the "we all's" had really begun to get under Casey's skin. She understood black people who spoke with a wayward dialect. Oppression had just about decimated their intellect. Yet many African Americans overcame their situation and were eloquent speakers. But Deborah had all the advantages in the world. Casey could have gone on for hours disparaging her brother and his fiancée, but she hugged them both and wished them a Merry Christmas.

As the three of them left Hal's home, Casey's mom Anne felt some tension, so she tried to relieve it by asking, "How's your friend in Seattle doing, Casey?" From the back seat of the Taurus, Casey could see her father stiffen. She knew her mother and father had different views of people, so Casey thought that she might as well play along with the situation.

"Well, Mom, Roger and I are doing well. We're getting serious, you know.

Anne said, "That's great, dear! Do you plan on bringing him to Philadelphia sometime soon?"

Casey looked at her father, who said nothing. Then, pointing the remark to her father, Casey said, "I'd like to, Mom, but Roger is having trouble with some people back in Seattle, and he's trying to figure out who's causing the trouble."

"That's too bad," Anne said. "I hope everything works out. By the way, Casey, how did you like visiting your little brother?"

Casey felt that her mom was either a consummate faker or she was as naive as a seven-year-old. "I really enjoyed it, Mom, especially when the rodents came out!"

"Oh, Casey, now give your brother credit. You know he's doing well for himself, considering."

"Yeah, he could have wound up locked away."

Eugene butted in at that point, saying, "Now see here young lady. You'll respect my sons, you hear?"

Feeling bitchy, Casey said, "Sure, Dad, anything you say."

However Eugene wasn't finished. "Just because a certain young lady hung onto her father's coattails doesn't give her the right to put down her family!"

"Eugene!" Anne said, hurt.

"Well, it's true." Eugene knew why he was angry. The name Roger had popped up, which was more than he could take at the moment.

Angered by her dad's remark, Casey said, "Well, I don't have to work for you, Dad."

"Fine, just quit. I always knew you were a quitter!"

"No, Dad, you'll have to fire me first!"

Eugene was driving fast now, and he wouldn't return the fireball Casey had just thrown at him. Instead, eyes forward while driving on the expressway, he concentrated hard on not to calling his daughter a nigger-loving bitch. He knew it would destroy Anne, so he held his tongue.

That night in her room, Casey packed her bags and decided to leave. It was 12:30 a.m. Eugene and Anne were in the kitchen drinking eggnog when Casey approached them. "I'm going back to Seattle tonight, and I was coming to say good-bye."

Anne spoke first, saying, "Don't leave yet, Casey. You've only been here two days."

"I know, Mom, but I have to leave. I'm feeling suffocated here."

Anne looked like she was ready to cry. She hadn't thought the friction between Eugene and Casey would go this far. She knew that Eugene was part of a hate group, and she could have kicked herself for not seeing—until now—what was right in front of her face. Roger might be a target of Eugene's hatred. Anne believed that Eugene had a certain level of decency. Would he stoop as low as to intimidate Casey's boyfriend—worse? After putting it all together in her mind, Anne was upset. "Well, Casey, do what you must, but I'll miss you, sweetheart." Casey and her mother hugged each other tightly. Casey didn't speak to her father, but wished her mother a Merry Christmas before calling a cab.

Eugene wasn't a dim-witted man, and he knew Anne could piece things together quite easily. But if Wilson got his letter and showed his loyalty to the Sheppards, Casey would eventually come to her senses and come crawling back to her father. If Wilson was not who he said he was, however, Eugene realized he'd have problems on his hands.

Casey

CHAPTER 6

CASEY'S

Casey made it back to Seattle despite the weather. It was snowing in Philadelphia, but she still managed to board a flight. After stopovers in Chicago and Albuquerque, she was furious about the strange flight plan. "You would think a person could get a nonstop flight to Seattle," she fumed. Casey had missed Roger, even thought they were only apart a couple of days. She didn't call him from home, concerned that her father might overhear the conversation.

When Casey arrived at her apartment, she was exhausted and ready to hit the sack. "That'll be forty bucks, young lady." The cab driver, no youngster, said this nonchalantly.

Casey, eyeing her heavy bags, said, "I'll throw in $10 more if you help me get my bags to the door."

"Sure thing, ma'am." The cabbie was thrilled at the prospect of some extra cash.

Casey thanked the elderly gentlemen, who had bad breath, but a genuine smile, and began unlocking her front door. Right then it opened.

"Roger!" Casey was surprised. "So, you've moved in."

I hugged her, and took her bags from the cabbie. We kissed quietly in the doorway. Casey then said, "Let me come in and get out of these clothes, so I can relax. Okay, sweetheart?"

"Sure, girl, let me help you." As I helped Casey undress, she realized that she had been traveling for over twenty-four hours. Too tired to go in and take a shower, she tried to crawl in bed, but I wouldn't let her.

"Come on, Roger, I need some rest. I haven't even showered."

I was pushing the issue. Casey could now feel my erection. I was trying to penetrate her through her panties! After several thrusts, Casey became excited. So she pulled her panties to one side and moaned with pleasure as I entered her.

With Christmas over, I awakened early. Casey was still sleeping soundly. I probably upset her with my antics when she arrived at the apartment, but I'd been ready to explode, and I had to relieve the tension. I'd been awake about thirty minutes when Charlotte came out of the spare room. She kissed me and said, "Well, Roger, I'll be leaving for rehab today in Salt Lake City. All I have to do is board the plane."

I made toast with raspberry jelly, and while my mom and I ate breakfast, I calculated my next move. I would try to see my mom off before I went to work. I'd see Casey later that day and would explain why my mom had been there. Mom and I had talked about the rehabilitation center she would be going to. It was called Destiny's Retreat. The center kept the clients there for three months at a cost of $15,000. Charlotte wasn't troubled by the sale of her home. Leon appeared to be legit. Now Charlotte had more than $60,000 to start over wherever she wanted to. I wouldn't take any money from my mother; she'd eventually need every penny.

As we left Casey's apartment and headed for the airport, my mother and I didn't quite know what to say to each other. Charlotte didn't want to ruin the newfound respect she enjoyed from Theo and the kids. They seemed to have been real happy to see her, and Charlotte wanted to keep it that way. "Roger, you know what I want to do when I go through rehab?"

"What's that, Mom?" I listened to my mother intently.

"I want to start my own beauty salon."

"That would be great, Mom. Maybe I can help you." This pleased Charlotte, who said, "I'd like that, son."

I turned on the radio, oblivious to the dismal weather, singing as I drove to the airport.

Eugene had sent the letter by Priority Mail. He was hoping Wilson had received it by now. If so, when he called Wilson, the younger man would know exactly what to do.

Earlier, Eugene had had his accountant check on his clothing store in Seattle. The accountant, Todd Lifton, told Eugene that his Seattle store had $50,000 in the checking account. Eugene was sure that the account balance should have been more than $200,000. Casey was clearly responsible for the theft, yet Eugene wasn't surprised.

"I would have done the same thing myself under the circumstances, Eugene said to himself, as he thought of the best way to sell the store property. Eugene had closed his Seattle-based clothing store and was waiting for someone to buy it. He had told Casey about the move, but he wasn't concerned about her now. Eugene was more interested in finding out what Allen Wilson had to say. Eugene dialed the number and waited.

The phone rang three times, then Wilson came on the line. "Allen speaking."

"Hi, Allen. This is Eugene Balkner."

Realizing who was on the line, Allen was nervous now, but he didn't want his nervousness to show. "Well, hello, Mr. Balkner."

"Call me Eugene. Did you get my letter?"

"Yes, I did, Eugene."

Eugene's spirits perked up. He then replied, "I don't want you to answer me now, but write me!"

Allen blurted out, "They're living together, Eugene!"

Eugene was caught completely off-guard. "When did this happen?"

Allen was on shaky ground with a man like Balkner and was trying to be careful. "He moved in while Casey was away. I did some snooping, and I saw him move in. He and another black woman."

Eugene gathered his thoughts before adding, "Good work, Wilson. I'll be in touch with you. Remember, I want your answer by mail." Eugene hung up and thought about what he had just learned. So she took the money, and she's living with that nigger. I have to be real careful now or else I could bring myself down, he thought. Then he plotted his next move.

Anne had started eavesdropping. on Eugene's calls. She picked up the conversation about Casey and Roger living together, and she was pleased about that. If Eugene were as calculating as Anne thought, he wouldn't do anything—at least by himself—to harm either one of them. As Eugene replaced the phone in its cradle, Anne quickly went to her room and pretended to be doing some cleaning.

Allen had to get in touch with Casey, so he decided to call her.

"Hello, Casey. This is Allen Wilson."

Casey sat up in bed and checked the time: 10:30 a.m. "Hello," she said sleepily.

"Sorry to wake you, but I have some information about your father." Casey perked up a little bit. "Let's meet at my apartment at noon. I'll be here, okay?"

"Okay, Casey. I'll be there."

After dropping my mother off at the airport, I contemplated things on my way to work. My mother had told me how she found Destiny's Retreat—her first call. She had reached Sue Brown, a receptionist at the center. Sue had been very polite to Charlotte, who in turn decided to go to Destiny's. Charlotte had to wire the money so she could be treated immediately. My cell phone rang, interrupting my thoughts about my mother. It was Casey.

"Roger, I'm having a meeting with Allen Wilson at noon, and I want you to be here."

"Okay, sweetheart, I'll take an early lunch and be there by noon. I want to hear from Mr. Wilson." Both Casey and I knew that Wilson had something important to tell us.

"I'll see you then. Okay, Roger. 'Bye."

"Later, sweetness."

As I shut off my cell phone, I thought about my next move. I would tell Mr. Gillione that I could work until 11:30 a.m., then I had some personal business to take care of. As I rounded the corner by the hotel, I noticed a group of police cars, dozens of people milling around, and yellow police tape. Then I saw Madeline standing by a policeman, crying uncontrollably. I quickly drove around the building to locate a parking spot. Afterwards, I hurried to Madeline, fighting my way through the crowd until I reached her.

"Hey, Madeline, what's going on?" I asked nervously.

Madeline seemed relieved to spot a familiar face. "Oh, Roger," she said sorrowfully. Then she fell into my arms.

A female police officer was courteous enough to me, but she said sternly, "Sir, don't go past the yellow line. This is police business!"

I was stunned. I replied meekly, "Okay, officer." I was still trying to comfort Madeline, who had calmed down a little.

"Roger," Madeline said, fighting for control, "someone killed Mr. Gillione and two other men who were in the hotel with him.

Shocked, I began wondering who would kill Mr. Gillione. Then I started putting two and two together. Mr. Gillione seemed to be a respectable enough citizen, but I knew otherwise.

As the police continued to investigate, I decided to try to get some answers. I took Madeline, put her into my car, and then went back to the crime scene. I stopped a plainclothes policeman. "Excuse me, officer. I'm Roger Singleton, and I'm an employee here. What's the problem?"

The officer, Hank Albright, looked me over, then decided that I was telling the truth. "Well, young man, there have been multiple murders here. It appears to be a robbery, but we're not satisfied. We have three bodies inside the building."

Hank Albright, a detective for over three years, was still wet behind the ears. But he figured that the young black man standing in front of him probably didn't have anything to do with this bloodbath; otherwise, I might have been brought in for questioning. "This your first time reporting to work Mr._____?"

"The name's Singleton, officer. Roger Singleton."

"Well Mr. Singleton, we're probably going to be here the rest of the morning. We have to gather evidence." Then Albright surprised me by saying, "Give me your phone number, Mr. Singleton, and I'll call you if something comes up or if we need you to answer some questions."

I sized up Albright, a rather tall, lean, hard-looking man. The detective had a boyish face, which was acne-scarred. His penetrating blue eyes would look right through a person. His voice commanded respect, yet he seemed to be a peaceful man. I got a kick out of his cheap blue suit. Finally, I spoke. "Here's my number, officer, and let me have yours, too."

This pleased Albright. "Okay, young man, but in the meantime, I suggest that you find somewhere else to hang around, okay?" The firm, yet respectful way Albright said this gave me no alternative but to comply.

Madeline was still in my car when I came back. She was smoking a cigarette to calm her nerves. Politely I said, "Could you please put that thing out, girl. They stink!"

Madeline quickly threw the cigarette out of the car. "Oh, alright, spoil sport." We both looked at each other and smiled sadly. Madeline spoke first. "So, what now, Roger?"

I eyed my coworker. "I don't know, Madeline, but let's stay in touch. Let's exchange phone numbers."

"That would be great, Roger. I'd like to stay in touch with you." We hugged and cried before we gave each other our phone numbers.

I dropped Madeline home, then sped over to Casey's apartment. Allen Wilson was already there. "Hello, Roger, nice to see you," Allen said as he met me at the door. We shook hands, and then Allen got back down to business.

"As I was saying, Casey, your father is very serious about things. He appears to be a racist, yet he's not doing the dirty work himself—he wants his followers to do that."

Fist clenched, I motioned for Allen to go on.

"Look, Roger, Mr. Balkner wants you dead!"

My heart seemed to jump out of my chest. "Dead!" I yelled instinctively. "Why dead?! I thought he wanted to rough me up a little bit, but dead! Damn."

Casey ran from the room, crying. Still stunned, I wanted to know more. "Just how does he want to have it done?"

Allen wouldn't say that Balkner had asked him to do the job; he didn't want to alarm us. For now, Allen just wanted to earn the money Casey was paying him. "Listen, Roger, Mr. Balkner is very serious and very determined. I'd be very careful if I were you."

I began to let everything sink in. Balkner wanted me dead. I understood that I was seeing a white woman and that it in itself was dangerous, but I was beginning to grasp the nature of interracial relationships in America. "Well, Allen, what else is going on with Mr. Balkner?" Allen went on, "I went to a meeting of Sheppards a week or so ago, and Balkner commanded the complete respect of the men there. The private investigator looked at me, sighed, turned his eyes upward, and continued. "I want to go to a few more meetings to get a feel for things. Anyway, try not to go to far from Casey; she's your protection."

I thought about what Allen had told us before I said. "I'll be careful, Allen—you can bet on that!"

Wilson got up to leave, checking out the neat, spacious, well-decorated apartment. Expensively designed, too. I wonder who's paying the bills, Allen thought as he walked out of the apartment.

Casey finally came out of her room, fighting the jet lag, She had put herself together.

"Roger, who was sleeping in the spare room?" she asked

"My mom. I had her stay here until I took her to the airport to fly to her rehabilitation center."

Casey was surprised at this. "Your mom's in rehab?"

"Yes, she is, Casey. Now what are we going to do about this situation?"

"I really don't know, Roger. I don't know." For the first time I realized what enemies could do to the mind.

Allen Wilson wrote Eugene a reply. He stated in the letter that he'd consider taking the assignment, but that it wouldn't be easy. Never before had be killed anyone in cold blood. Allen still needed to investigate the Sheppards. It was one thing to be in a hate group, but being solicited to commit a murder—that was entirely different.

I told Casey what had happened to Mr. Gillione. She was shocked. It was nearly six o'clock in the evening, so I turned on the local news. As we watched the news together, the story finally came on. The newscaster reported from the scene. "At about seven a.m. this morning, an employee discovered the grizzly scene of three men shot to death. Authorities say that it might have been gang related." I turned off the television set, and whispered. "So they knew about Gillione."

Casey said, "Roger, I suspect that you're doing something underhanded. What is it?"

I didn't want to lie to my lady, but I didn't want trouble, either. "Casey, I have my moments, but I'm not so terrible. One day I'll tell you, sweetheart."

Casey had enough tension for the day. "I'm going to get some rest, Roger. You coming? Whatever it is you're doing, I hope you're not involved with your ex-boss!"

I let out a sigh of relief that I wasn't in cahoots with Gillione. Both Casey and I headed for the bedroom.

Through his sources, Eugene found out that Casey had indeed taken the money out of the store's account. So Casey had gotten away with that one. He wasn't mad about it; he just counted it as a loss. Patiently he waited for Allen Wilson's letter. Things would change for that nigger-loving daughter of his. For now Eugene had some time on his hands.

The meeting that night for the Seattle Sheppards went well. After the meeting, Allen Wilson quickly left the premises. He didn't want to spread himself too thin so soon. He hadn't heard anything new or particularly interesting. For the most part, it seemed that the meetings were designed to collect dues and to give members a chance to socialize. In order to find out more about the Sheppards, Allen would have to be initiated into the group. For now, he wanted to play the role of an interested prospective member.

Casey

CHAPTER 7

THE ISLAND

Eugene had received Allen Wilson's reply some time ago. Wilson had seemed to be speaking the truth. Now Eugene wanted to know if Wilson was a plant or if he was legit. He'd put Wilson in with a group of seasoned followers of the Sheppards. They, in turn, would figure out how to do away with Roger Singleton, and Eugene would be nowhere around. That would teach Casey to go against his wishes. Eugene started making phone calls.

Eugene began to think things through. He had become a self-made millionaire. His eight retail stores in the United States had earned him over $5 million. Even with closing his store in Seattle, Eugene still earned over $250,000 a year. He'd felt confident letting Casey run his store in Seattle. She had proved more than up to the task; he even considered putting her in charge of several of his other stores—until she began dating that Roger Singleton.

Eugene felt that he tolerated people of color well enough, but he knew that oppression and poverty had turned many of them into outright thieves, not at all trustworthy. Over the years, Eugene had even hired a dozen or so minority employees. They didn't give Eugene trouble, but he had made sure his top people kept an eye on them. He didn't hate Casey, but she had really thrown a wrench into his plans. Now he had to decide what to do. Not only was Roger dating his daughter, but he was trampling on Eugene's worldview. Casey's dad could tolerate having inferiors work for him, but he refused to welcome them as family. That was taking it too far. Besides, what would the Sheppards think?

They had to work hard to guide their respective communities. In Eugene's opinion, people could not look out for themselves. They had to have leaders who could look out for their best interests. And letting someone with Roger's background find out about the work of the Sheppards was dangerous. He might let word leak out. God forbid that the public became aware of the Sheppards. That's the last thing Eugene wanted—to have reporters nosing around the meetings.

Eugene felt that he could trust Allen Wilson, but he wasn't a hundred percent sure. Wilson had appeared out of nowhere and seemed to be a calculating man. Wilson's eyes exuded a thoughtful intelligence. This worried Eugene. Even more worrisome was Wilson's reply, describing himself as a nonviolent man—that wasn't what Eugene had expected. No white man should be nonviolent, Eugene believed. It was against white U.S. history. As long as Eugene could remember, the white man had been fighting for survival. Unless Wilson was religious or a vegetarian, Eugene wouldn't accept his being soft. He would get in touch with the senior members of the Sheppards in Seattle, and have them work with Allen Wilson. Eugene felt the sleep hit his eyes and decided to take a nap.

Anne had told Eugene that she had some shopping to do and would be home a little late. She knew Philadelphia time was ahead of Seattle's, so she called Casey on her cell as quickly as she could. No one answered the phone, so Anne left a message. "Hello, Casey? Sweetheart, this is Mom. Casey, I know you're a careful person, but watch your step, young lady, and tell Roger to be careful, too. I love you sweetheart." Crying softly, Anne hung up the phone.

Anne had grown to admire her husband over the years. She didn't harbor any romantic love for Eugene, but she had given him three children. Now over fifty, Anne looked decent enough. Sure, her breasts were sagging a bit and she had a slight tummy. Still, men would give her a second glance when she passed by. She was still an attractive woman.

Eugene had suggested plastic surgery, but Anne wouldn't have it. No one was going to cut her unless it was absolutely necessary. She'd just have to live with the slight bags under her eyes. Putting aside troubling thoughts about her family, Anne picked up the pace to get her shopping done.

Casey played back her messages. The one from her mom had upset her. Mom never went against Dad, but the message sounded like Anne was worried about her. She and I were trying to decide what we could do to relax after this spate of bad news. A trip to Bainbridge Island might cheer us up. I hadn't been on a vacation in some time. Mr. Gillione had become a real friend to me, and keeping busy was one of the things I had enjoyed about working at the hotel.

I had already called my dad and explained the situation about the killings. Dad was more worried about me than about Mr. Gillione, yet he felt for Gillione's family. I knew that Mr. Gillione had been involved with illegal activities. The errands I ran for him gave me more reason to worry.

"Roger, I'm almost finished packing. What about you?" Casey anxiously asked, more than ready for the trip.

"Yes, Casey, I packed a few things, so whenever you're ready, let's go."

We practically sprinted for my car. I went back to lock the door and then we were off. We planned to spend a few hours on Bainbridge Island. With the weather still cold, Bainbridge, one of the more popular islands, wouldn't be crowded. We decided to take my car, because it was more economical. We were both thrilled to be outdoors-it was a refreshing relief from the bustle of the city. The choppy waters on the ferry ride across to Bainbridge made the ferry sway gently, and prompted both of us to lovingly cling to each other. Oblivious to the other riders, we shared several passionate kisses. Casey couldn't wait to sample some of the great seafood at Winslow Way. It was her way of relieving stress. I, on the other hand, just wanted to get away for a spell.

After spending several hours on the island, we began to get weary. We held hands as we walked and talked about our dilemma. Casey and I decided to call it a day, but not before savoring a sumptuous meal. The island offered delicious food that wasn't available on the mainland.

A little more relaxed about things now, Casey was ready to head home. On the ferry back, Casey eyed me, then said, "Roger, what will you do about a job, now?"

"I'm not sure, but I'll do something."

Casey didn't want to tell me about the money she'd taken. I might just decide to rely on her for everything. "Well, anyway, rent is still due at the end of each month, and I don't have a job either."

"What happened to your job, Casey?" I asked, surprised.

"My dad closed the business because of us." I was taken aback.

"Your father really has it in for me, doesn't he, girl?"

For some reason, Casey was feeling good about things, in spite of her father. "Don't worry, Roger, we'll get by."

I shrugged my shoulders and prepared for the ride across the bay.

There were three messages on Casey's answering machine. Casey listened to them all, but she was intrigued by the call from the Seattle Police Department. They wanted to talk to me as soon as possible. The other two—from Allen Wilson and Casey's mom—would have to wait. Casey quickly summoned me from the bathroom. "Roger, the police need to talk to you right away." I stiffened a little. "I have the number of a policeman by the name of Hank Albright. He's a detective. I'll give him a call."

I had almost forgotten where I'd put the telephone number Albright had given me. I went to the kitchen and dialed the detective's number.

"Detective Albright, Seattle Police Department."

"Hello, detective. This is Roger Singleton. I was asked to call you."

"Yes, Mr. Singleton. I need you to come down to the station."

I can come in tomorrow morning. Is that okay?" I was a bit apprehensive, now thinking about my crack dealing.

"Eight o'clock, okay?"

"Sounds good to me, detective. I'll be there."

"Good deal. See you then, Roger."

I hung up the phone. My days as a crack dealer would have to end. I had flushed about a hundred dollars' worth of drugs down the toilet after Gillione's murder. If the Seattle police knew anything about my drug distribution business, they had said nothing. I had never been in trouble with the law, and I considered myself very fortunate on that score. In a city like Seattle, it wasn't every day that a black youth grew up without a record. I credited Mr. Gillione with keeping me out of trouble. The job at the Haven had given me credibility, and Mr. Gillione always covered for me whenever I needed help. I had a little over $3,000 stashed away. I hadn't wanted to get in touch with Chu because of the threats from Casey's father. There was no telling how closely Eugene had been watching me.

That night in bed, I tossed and turned. Sleep wouldn't be come easily. I kept visualizing what Mr. Gillione did. I knew Mr. Gillione skirted the law, but I couldn't pinpoint his illegal activities. Then I thought of Madeline and checked the time. It was 1:30 in the morning. I jumped out of bed and ran into the kitchen. I stumbled over a few things in the darkness, but I managed to make it in one piece.

Madeline was groggy, but she answered the phone. "Hello?"

"Madeline, this is Roger. I need to ask you a few questions."

She woke up slightly and said, "Can you come over right now? I don't like talking on the phone."

"I'll try, Madeline, but that might be difficult."

Madeline understood the difficulties of explaining to one's significant other the need to leave home in the middle of the night. "It's the only way, Roger." Then she hung up.

I decided to tell Casey the truth. She was a little angry at first, then decided to come along. Not wanting to create a scene with my lady, I didn't object. The ride over to Madeline's was quiet. It had been raining continuously. I didn't like driving at this time of night, especially with police breathing down my neck, and the ride seemed like an eternity. I was glad that Casey was with me; she knew the area better than I did.

Arriving at Madeline's near East Madison Street, I was sure I'd aged a couple of years in the time it took to drive there. As and Casey and I got out of the car, we both looked around nervously. The coast seemed clear. I knocked lightly on the door several times. Madeline finally opened it. Casey and I entered the dimly lit hallway, and Madeline ushered the two of us into the kitchen.

"Come on, guys. It's all the way in the back."

I walked into the kitchen, and saw a man sitting at the kitchen table. It was Albright. "Hello, Roger. I thought I might run into you here. How are you?"

I didn't know what to say, so I just nodded my head.

"Have a seat, Roger. We need to talk."

I was getting nervous now. My throat began drying up. "Can I have a glass of water, Madeline?" I asked as I looked at her menacingly.

Madeline shrugged her shoulders and through body motions signaled, what else could I do?

I then turned my attention back to Albright. "Now what's this all about?" I looked right at Albright, who tried to relax me.

"Take it easy, young fella. I just want to ask you a simple question."

"Okay, go ahead." I sighed.

"Have you ever done anything for Mr. Gillione besides working at the hotel?" I wanted to lie, but I'd always wondered how Mr. Gillione kept the hotel open with the few customers he catered to.

"Well, detective, 1 did run errands for Mr. Gillione on many occasions—delivering packages. I didn't ask questions. I only did what he asked me to do."

"What was in the packages, Roger?" Albright asked sternly.

"I believe it was cash." I might be charged with money laundering, but I didn't know what else to say. Then I said, "Look, detective, I feel like I've been set up. I mean I called Madeline just to see if she knew anything, so I would have information for our meeting tomorrow." Then I asked, "What brings you here anyway?"

Albright felt the tension in my question. "Look, son, we know that Mr. Gillione was laundering money through several of his establishments." Albright let that sink in.

I was stunned. Mr. Gillione? Such a nice man on the surface how could he . . .? Hank Albright read people well, and he saw that I hadn't been aware of the scope of Gillione's operation. Albright continued, "Also, Mr. Gillione was suspected in several murders in Miami. We found that out through an informant. Now, Mr. Singleton, is there anything else you want to tell me—anything at all?" Albright drummed his fingers on the table, waiting for an answer. I had to say something so I decided to reveal the relationship Madeline had with Gillione. "Well, detective, I know that Madeline and Mr. Gillione were lovers."

Hank Albright sat up straight in his chair and directed his next question to Madeline. "Is that true, young lady?" Madeline gave me a murderous look and tried to compose herself.

"Yes, Mr. Albright, we were. But I was only something on the side for Mr. Gillione, that's all."

The detective couldn't press charges for sexual relations, but he could hold her for withholding information. Albright felt that these two had no motive to kill Gillione. According to reports, Gillione was a shrewd man who would never divulge too much information to his employees. "Okay, you two, I'll be in touch. If I need any more information, I'll call. And stay out of trouble."

Both Madeline and I chimed in together, "We will, detective!"

Hank Albright stood up to leave and said good-bye to the ladies. He then walked out of the apartment.

Madeline playfully hit me on the arm. "Why did you say that, Roger?"

I was angry, "Why did you have the cop here waiting for me like that?" Madeline looked away sheepishly, then said, "Well, what else could I do? He asked me to do it."

"Well, Madeline, if we get charged, at least it won't be for murder." Madeline turned to Casey, who had sat motionless through the whole ordeal. "Are you okay?" Madeline asked, concerned.

"Casey, Casey Balkner. How are you?"

"I'm fine, and I guess you know by now that my name is Madeline." Both girls shook hands. "Can I get you something, Casey?"

63

"No, I'm fine, thanks."

I said, "Hey, we'd better get going, Casey. It's pretty early in the morning. I could still get some rest."

Madeline showed us both to the door before saying, "Keep in touch, Roger."

"I will, girl. See you later."

As Casey and I left Madeline's apartment, Casey had plenty of questions. Surprisingly, she said almost nothing on the way home. I was worried, and when we got in the bedroom I asked, "You okay, Casey? You're very quiet."

"I'm fine Roger, I was just thinking about a phone call that came in earlier. Allen Wilson wants us to call him."

"What time is it, Casey? Maybe we could call him right now."

Casey dialed the number, and Allen answered, "Yes?" He sounded sleepy, but courteous and professional nonetheless.

"Hello, Allen, this is Casey Balkner. You called earlier."

Allen sat up in bed. "Yes, Casey. I needed to know if you wanted to continue with this investigation. I've learned what it is you already suspected, and if you like, I can close the case."

"Will you go to the authorities?"

"Not until an attempt is made on Roger's life, and then you'd have to decide if you wanted to press charges."

Allen Wilson's fees were high, but Casey still needed him. "I want to keep you on the case, Allen. Can you continue?"

"Yes I can, but I'm going to need a payment."

"Sure. I'll bring to your office first thing tomorrow."

"Good. Next time, Miss Balkner, please call during work hours."

"Sorry, Allen, and good morning."

"Good-bye, Miss Balkner."

Casey hung up, and then listened to her mother's message again. Her mother sounded worried, but she definitely wanted to warn Casey.

Casey thought about her situation. I was out of work, and so was she. The clothing store job was over—her dad had made sure of that. If only she could find something to do until things got better. This was the worst holiday season she'd ever been through, and she was glad it was over. "Move over, Roger," she muttered as she climbed into bed.

"Okay, boss." Casey wasn't in a good mood, so I refrained from commenting about everything we were facing now. It was worth it to help the man she loved, Casey thought, but this was going to take a lot of love. Besides, she needed to stop her father from running her life. With her eyes getting heavy, Casey finally drifted into a fitful sleep.

Allen

CHAPTER 8

THE FIGHT

After arriving at Allen's office and looking around, Casey started wondering if she'd made the right decision coming here. Hopefully no one saw me or followed me, she mused to herself as she knocked on Allen's tinted glass office door. Allen opened the door moments later.

"Well, hello, Miss Balkner. Come in."

"Thanks, Allen." Casey then strode into the small office. She looked over the place, which was very neat, with photos of large fish held by happy fishermen hanging on every wall. Otherwise, the diminutive office had a desk, which was slightly cluttered, two chairs, and a small bookcase in the corner of the room. Casey spoke first. "Can I sit down?"

"Why, sure. Pardon my rudeness." For the first time Allen noticed how attractive Casey was. His senses heightened, yet he tried to maintain his professionalism. "So, Casey, I've got to the root of the problem. Your father wants Roger eliminated." He waited for a reply, smiling at Casey with a practiced eye.

Casey noticed Allen's subtle flirting, but decided to ignore it. "I want to stop my father from hurting Roger. Is there any way you could do that?"

Allen's curiosity was piqued: Most clients would have been happy to learn the important facts of a case and then turn it over to the authorities. What was Casey Balkner's angle? Did she want to kill her father? "I don't understand you, Casey," Allen said, genuinely perplexed.

"Well," Casey went on, "I may not take your evidence and go to the police right now, but I do want to have enough proof so I can stop the actions of Dad's group."

This was case of an altogether different magnitude. To stop an organization like the Sheppards, you needed more than a small-time private eye; you needed a small army. Allen tried to reason with Casey. "Look, I can do more digging, but this may get dangerous for me. If the Sheppards find out about me, kaboom. I'm a dead man."

She listened intently, but felt compelled to push the issue. "Look, Allen, I can find someone else. I mean I realize that you're putting yourself in harm's way, but I have something at stake here, too."

"I understand," Allen replied somberly.

The PI had mixed feelings about this business. He respected people of color; they had helped build America and make the country strong. He also thought that this attractive white woman was paying an awful lot of money for an unproven man. Sure, Roger was a smart kid. He may even be a romantic guy, but relationships started and ended every day, and to spend this kind of money on this kind of risky venture was not terribly wise. So Allen tried to reason with her. "Look, all I'm saying that maybe you're letting your emotions get ahead of your reasoning. You seem like a bright woman. Why don't you find a nice guy? You know, one you have more in common with." Casey knew exactly what Allen meant.

"You mean like a nice, sweet, white man."

"Well," Allen hesitated, "yes." Casey wasn't mad; she'd play along for a while.

"Like you, Allen?"

"Maybe."

Intrigued by his honesty, Casey said, "You know, Allen, if I hadn't met Roger before you came along, then I wouldn't have to pay for your services. We could just screw our brains out." Allen knew he was outclassed, and he didn't want to push it. "Okay, I understand love when I run across it. It never makes any sense, but problems always bring out character. You know what I mean?"

Both Casey and Allen had been thoroughly engaged in the conversation. Leaning back in her chair, Casey said, "I'm not doing this out of love. I'm doing it out of obligation. What right does my father have to harm Roger? Roger has the same rights as any other citizen. Killing him for being a man is despicable!"

Allen stood up to face Casey. "I'm just saying that dealing with a guy like your father is very risky. I can stay on the case, even risking my own life, but here's my main concern: What if your father comes after you?"

Casey wasn't prepared for that. "My dad is a volatile person, and he and I have had words. . ." Casey was more amused at that thought than frightened.

"Okay," Allen said. "I need an advance. I need it in the neighborhood of $5,000." Pleased, Casey took out her checkbook. "How's $20,000, Allen? And, oh, as long as it takes to stop my dad from trying to control things."

Allen smiled, thinking that Casey was way out of her league. As Casey handed him the check, he shook her hand. "Thank you, Casey. I'll be in touch."

"Fine. Keep me posted, Allen." As she rose to leave, Allen stopped her.

"Casey, wait." Allen decided to tell her where things stood. "Your father wants *me* to kill Roger!"

Stunned, Casey whispered, "Why you?"

"They're testing me to see if I'm Sheppard material." Allen didn't know the full rationale behind Eugene's plan, but he had to keep both Casey and Eugene on a tight string.

Casey wanted to give the PI an out. "Maybe you should get off the case. Maybe we should go to the authorities."

Allen looked at Casey wistfully, and suddenly stroked her hair. "Your father's a shrewd man. He'd wiggle out of it real quick. Let's just keep our fingers crossed, okay?"

"Alright. I hope you'll be safe." She reached for Allen, and they shared a fear-induced kiss. They lingered in the embrace for just a moment before Casey stepped back and abruptly said, "Good-bye, Allen."

"Take care, Casey." Allen let his hand slide all the way to Casey's waist. Casey didn't protest, but she hastily turned and left.

Allen considered his next move. He was planning to go to a meeting that night and talk with Leo Simon. Now that Casey wanted him to continue on the case, he had to come up with a strategy, one that would buy him enough time to persuade Casey either to confront her father or to go to the authorities. Either way, he'd have to do his homework. The PI gathered several items, along with Casey's check, and quietly left his secluded office near Jackson Street. Well away from the Sheppards.

When Allen arrived at home, he carefully concealed the check Casey had given him. If that check were spotted by the Sheppards—Allen shuddered at the thought. Once he deposited the check, the money would tide him over for at least three months, since he didn't plan on spending large sums of money on anything too soon.

Allen checked his messages; his brother William had called from Cleveland. William was also a private eye, but he was seven years older than Allen and had been in the business much longer. Allen didn't dare bring William into this case, even though he wanted to consult with his brother about it. Allen listened to the message. "Hello, little brother, I was thinking about you and I thought I'd give you a ring. The wife and kids are doing fine. Hope to hear from you soon. See you."

William was a savvy private investigator and could give him sound advice. The Seattle PI pondered calling his brother, and then thought better of it. He didn't want to get into a lengthy conversation—not right now, anyway. Instead, he'd shower and take a nap. He had a very busy day ahead of him.

At seven that night, Allen walked into the meeting. Every Monday night, the Sheppards met on 34th Street. Tonight, Leo Simon was leading the meeting. "Good evening, gentlemen. I want to welcome all of you to tonight's meeting. I hope all is well with everyone. . ." Allen noticed the almost boring way in which Simon addressed the group. A handsome man, Simon was of medium height with a neatly trimmed beard and rich, dark hair. Simon had a square jawline, which gave him a commanding presence. He wore a brown sports jacket with beige slacks, an odd combination, in Allen's view.

Simon was totally immersed in his own rhetoric. "Now listen, fellows, we know that our meeting here tonight is to keep us informed and to keep money matters in order. But tonight, gentlemen, we have some new business. I received a special call from Eugene Balkner." Simon looked around the room, noting that he was getting an anticipated silent approval from the group. "Tonight I propose that we accept Allen Wilson into our group." Allen sat there, stunned. "All in favor, say aye." The group said, "Aye!" Simon turned to the secretary, Terrence Hulbert, and said, "Record Allen Wilson as an official member of the Sheppards."

Terrence, a dark-haired, choirboy type, replied, "Consider it done, Mr. Simon."

Simon went over to Allen. "What do you think, Allen?"

Scared, nervous, and worried, the new recruit replied as enthusiastically as he could. "That sounds great, Mr. Simon!"

Leo knew from experience that Allen would probably be placed with the lower-echelon members, since he didn't seem to be cut from the same cloth as the members here. "By the way, Allen, I'm curious. How on earth did you find us?"

Allen didn't miss a beat, saying, "I didn't find out about you, I stumbled on the place. I figured this was a fishermen's club or something, but to my surprise . . ."

Leo wasn't totally convinced, but he didn't want to needle the young man Eugene had singled out. Leo wondered why Eugene didn't have one of the more experienced boys take care of that nigger Roger. Why go to all this trouble? Anyway, Leo decided to take Wilson out for coffee and explain things to him.

"Say, Allen, why don't we go for a cup of coffee?"

Allen thought about it for a moment and then angrily replied, "Why don't we talk right here, since you want to make all the decisions for me!"

"Now hold on, young man. Remember, you came to us!" Leo was seeing another side of the easygoing Allen Wilson. He tried to simmer things down. "Okay, Allen, take it easy. Let's stay here and have a cup of coffee."

Allen realized that he couldn't come to a meeting and sit by idly, doing nothing. Both men went to get coffee and then sat down and waited for the building to empty out.

Leo spoke first. "I want you to go to our training camp and learn more about what we do. OK?"

Allen knew that he had to play along. "Okay, Leo. When do I begin the training?"

"Well, we want to take you to one of our training camps on the outskirts of the Willapa Hills. Once you're there, we'll teach you a few things."

Allen was now in way over his head, but he had to roll with the punches. "So, this is what you wanted to talk to me about Leo—training?"

"Why, yes. Evidently, Eugene Balkner has taken a liking to you."

"Eugene—how could I forget," Allen said as kindly as possible.

Then Leo looked around the room to make sure that no one was listening and practically whispered to Allen, "By now I know you've heard what Eugene wants from you and, personally, I feel that he's being unreasonable. You know, Allen, it's not the main function of the Sheppards to go around killing black people. We do have our standards. I think Eugene is a little hot-headed, but he's a good man. Plus being a supreme leader is sometimes hard." Leo then patted Allen on the knee.

Allen had to remain nonchalant to maintain his cover. During the whole conversation, Leo was watching Allen's reactions very closely.

I met Chu at the Haven, as Chu had requested. Chu had called me the night of the murders. We shook hands and began walking. We came to a local fish shack and went inside. The place was half-empty and a little messy. Leftover food was still on some of the tables, and so were beer bottles. The waitresses looked tired and drawn. The reason Chu chose this place was that it catered to drifters, and no one paid much attention to the customers. Chu motioned for me to sit at one of the few clean tables in the place. A waitress came over, an overweight woman of about thirty with heavy makeup and short, dark hair. She had an "I could care less" attitude, and it showed in her voice. "What can I get you guys?"

Chu smiled and said, "Two Buds and an order of shrimp, please, Claudia."

"Sure thing, handsome. Comin' right up." Claudia then sauntered away.

"Just like I like it Roger—nice and quiet." Chu then studied me before saying, "So, Roger, I see you've been quiet. I haven't done any business with you for quite a while. Everything okay?"

"Sure, Chu. Just trying not to step on my own toes. You know my boss at the hotel was killed, don't you?"

Chu looked around and when he was absolutely sure the coast was clear, said, "Yeah, that guy. He tried to get in the game, Roger, but with the wrong people. He tried to walk over the Chinese players."

I let that sink in. So that's what happened to Gillione, I thought. "What did he do, Chu?" Roger asked, not expecting an answer.

"Well, he ordered a shipment of heroin from back East, down in Miami, two hundred pounds of the stuff. Only after he got the merchandise, he tried to muscle my boys by not paying.

"Whew," I said. "I always said that people who played with fire would get burned."

The waitress came back and placed the food and drinks on the table. "Here you go, guys."

"Thanks, Claudia," Chu said and patted her on the rear end. Claudia playfully shrieked and walked away, smiling at Chu.

"Have you hit that, Chu?" I said, almost bursting with laughter.

"Naw, I just let her play with my love thang, dude!"

I was amazed at Chu, yet I felt a little uneasy knowing about Gillione. "Anyway, Chu, what's up?"

"I think I'm getting ready for a huge shipment, and I need somebody to help distribute it. Just make deliveries with me and collect the money. We'll count it, and it will be worth your while."

I thought about it before saying, "Chu, the heat is on me because of Gillione, I hope you realize that."

"I do, Roger, and believe me, I wouldn't ask you if it meant getting busted."

"Yeah, Chu, I'm interested, but I'm living with my girl and she may go ballistic if she finds out."

Chu was quiet for a moment. Then he said, "I have a custodial business, Roger, and it's completely legit. All I have to do is hire you, and then we can take care of business, my man."

Flabbergasted, I said, "I didn't know you had a cleaning business, Chu. Damn!" I felt a renewed sense of hope. I even took a swig of beer. "You know, Chu, I hit on some shit a few weeks back and let me tell you, I won't ever try it again."

Chu gave me a hard, terrifying look. "Never mix business with pleasure, my friend. It's bad for your life."

Point well taken. Chu then decided it was time to leave the foul-smelling restaurant.

Kent Gardener and Kyle Mitchell were in the front seat. Tim Sanders and Mel Rose were in the back. The four men were riding around and drinking, looking for prostitutes. "Pass me another beer!" Kent said, as he wheeled around the corner.

"Sure, Kent," Mel said, handing him the brew. The streets were half-empty. There were no prostitutes out tonight. The men were followers of the Sheppards; they had just come from a meeting and were trying to relax. As Kent drove along the boulevard slowly, he spotted a black man. "Hey, you guys. That looks like Roger Singleton." Kent had met Eugene Balkner, who had shown him and a few other members a medium-sized photo of me.

"Stop the damn car!" Mel yelled. Kent quickly pulled over to the curb. The four men then downed their beers and stepped out of the car onto the curb. Chu and I noticed the four men getting out of the car, but didn't make the connection. We were about to go our separate ways, when all of a sudden the four men raced up to us.

"Hey, Roger, I got something for you!"

"You know these guys, Roger?" Chu asked, agitated.

"Not really," I replied, quite nervous now.

The four thugs set upon us. Kent Gardener, the biggest of the group, got in my face. "Hey, nigger. Goin' some place?"

"Yeah, home if you don't mind Woody."

"The name's Kent, but I guess savages don't use real names."

"Excuse me!" I replied harshly and tried to walk past the men.

"Hold it, Singleton. Who's the Chinaman?"

Chu was trying to stay out of it. He didn't need the trouble. So he said, "It looks like you boys have had a few too many drinks. So let's call it a night, alright?"

"Shut up, Chink boy!" Mel yelled, glaring at Chu. The four men surrounded us. Kent Gardener, the meanest one, swung and hit me in the left eye. I went down screaming. A low masculine scream, but it was obvious that I was in pain. Mel Rose then tried to kick me in the ribcage. It was a glancing blow that barely nicked me. Tim Sanders gave me a left-right combination to the jaw. To their surprise, I staggered to my feet and began swinging. I caught Tim in the groin, a low blow that landing him on his back.

Not knowing what else to do, Chu reflexively got into his Oriental fighting stance. Mel, ignoring it, charged Chu. This was a big mistake. Chu jumped in the air, kicked Mel in the face, and then gave him several more closed-fist blows to the head. Mel went down, holding his head in pain.

Meanwhile, Kyle Mitchell and Kent Gardener were working me over. Kyle was behind me, pinning my arms while Kent was gut-punching me.

Chu ran over to Kent and kicked him right between the shoulder blades. Kent dropped to his knees. Chu then gave Kyle three quick jabs to the face. Kyle held his arms up in surrender. Mel recovered enough to yell out, "Let's go guys. Forget it!" The two men left standing went over to Tim and Kent and helped them up, but, for good measure, I ran after them and struck Mel with a vicious blow to the back of the head. He staggered forward, but didn't turn around.

Still groggy, I went back to Chu. "Damn, Chu. Thanks, man. Whew!"

As the four men got back into their car, they were abuzz with anger. Kent started the car and then looked in the glove compartment and pulled out a nine millimeter. Chu and I were still standing there talking as Kent drove by. He took aim and fired eight shots toward us. Chu and I hugged asphalt as the bullets ripped past us. Kent then hit the accelerator and quickly sped away. Chu stood up first. Knees shaking, Chu helped me to my feet. My left eye badly swollen, I said, "I think I soiled my pants."

"I wouldn't blame you, my friend." People started getting closer and closer now, trying to figure out what was going on. "Let's get out of here, Roger." We quickly left the scene, heading for our cars.

I looked in the mirror after I showered. I hurt all over. My left eye was swollen shut. Must have been those damn Sheppards, I thought, as I dried myself off. Chu and I had almost lost our lives tonight. I pondered Chu's proposition. Helping Casey financially while still making a hustle was something I could handle. So Gillione had tried to muscle the Chinese out of their money. He really was a hard case, I mused. I knew not to mention what Chu had said to anybody.

Casey had been expecting trouble, so she was happy that I was still alive. Never mind the bruises and the eye swollen shut. As I came out of the bathroom, Casey gave me an ice pack. "Put this over your eye. It may help with the swelling."

"Alright. I hope it also helps with the pain," I said, as I placed the pack on my injured eye.

"Roger, you will just have to be more careful, sweetheart," Casey said, as she took another look at that eye.

"Yeah, but those white boys didn't know what hit them."

"So, who helped you, Roger?" Casey asked, curious.

"A friend of mine who happened to be in the area." I wasn't about to tell Casey about Chu. I'd never hear the end of it.

"Well, Roger, I have some good news."

"I could use some right about now."

"I'm the new saleswoman at McMurry's, a new clothing store in the city."

"I'm impressed, Casey." I limped over and kissed my girl. "I'm glad you're not depending on your dad any longer. He's really touched a nerve.

"Me, too."

Casey and I gave each other a knowing stare. She then came over to me and opened my bathrobe. "Just checking to make sure you don't have any damaged goods." I chuckled at her brashness and embraced my lady.

Mel kept checking his rearview mirror. The police weren't following them, so he relaxed a little. "Well, boys, I guess we got a taste of Roger Singleton tonight."

"Yeah!" yelled Kent Gardener, who still smarted from the blow he had taken.

The men were driving around the city, making sure they weren't being tailed by anyone. They were all dressed in blue jeans and fatigue jackets. All of them knew that Eugene Balkner had it in for Roger. They might have earned a little reward if they'd roughed him up some more, but they hadn't expected the Chinaman to come to the nigger's aid.

"Boy, if it wasn't for that Chink, Singleton would be dead," Mel said through clenched teeth as he angrily steered the car. Tim Sanders was deep in thought in the back seat. For now he'd keep massaging his testicles, which were still throbbing in pain.

Allen

CHAPTER 9

THE CAMP

The spring weather was mild—a welcome surprise. Casey had been doing well as a salesperson. Business was good, and she was even talking about opening her own retail business. Her father had stopped speaking to her, but she knew he wasn't finished with Roger. As she went over the day's take, she thought about Allen.

He had told her that he had been selected to kill Roger. It had been several months since she'd last spoken to him. At that point, he was supposed to be undergoing some type of training. Her dad was going all out in his zeal to get Roger. Casey giggled at the childish way her dad was behaving. He really should grow up, she thought, as she finished up for the day.

She'd go home and make a nice dinner for Roger. He'd begun working with a friend of his in the custodial business. Casey was thrilled that Roger was earning enough money to help her with the bills. At first her neighbors were uneasy about a black man living so close to them, but they had apparently gotten used to his smooth behavior. Casey closed the store and headed for her car. She remembered Roger telling her that he'd cut that dummy down from the tree in his front yard, and figured things were over and would probably get better. Little did he know. Casey would have liked to talk to her dad, but Eugene was a very stubborn and driven person. He'd stop at nothing. Casey remembered Allen's words. What if Eugene came after her? Casey continued driving, haunted by that image.

When Casey opened the door, I had already prepared dinner.

"Hello honey. What's for dinner?" Casey asked, giving me a kiss and pinching me on the butt.

"I cooked one of my mother's favorite meals—meatloaf, tossed salad, baked potatoes, and gravy."

"Well, it smells great. I can't wait!" Casey said, sitting down at the table. "No candles or romantic music tonight?"

"Well, I wanted to finish up before you got in. Excuse me."

"Let's eat, sweetheart," Casey replied hungrily.

Both Casey were seated now, and I said grace.

My eye had healed. I hadn't had any trouble with the Sheppards for a couple of months. I had begun carrying my thirty-eight special, just in case. The money I was making from Chu was great. I kept my stash in my Sunbird at home. My father and sisters always welcomed me there, and I was thrilled that my mother would be back from rehab soon.

Working at night was fine. Chu and I legitimately cleaned a dozen businesses each night, and then I'd ride shotgun while Chu made his deliveries. Usually, we ran into little or no trouble. No one liked messing with Chu, and I understood why. The man was like a rattler, poised to strike. I'd just play it cool, work with Chu, and try to keep Casey happy.

As we were eating, I asked, "When are we going to hear from Allen Wilson again, Casey?"

"I'm waiting for him to get back to me again. You know he has to be very careful."

I wanted to know what tricks the Sheppards were up to. "Well, Casey, you'll keep me posted?"

"Of course I will." As we finished eating, we gazed into each other's eyes. With the dishes still on the table, we made a beeline for the bedroom.

The Sheppards had forged a small military compound in the Willapa Hills. Allen was one of several dozen people at the camp. They ate three meals a day and played war games for three hours a day. The war games consisted mainly of sniper fire and engaging enemy fire, and they lounged around a lot after the exercises, speaking of white power. Allen knew this was their brainwashing technique.

They even had a firing range. Allen was instructed on how to use an M16 rifle. This lightweight weapon was one Allen learned to respect. Its accuracy impressed him. If I were doing this for sport, I'd probably buy one of these, he thought. He was taught to shoot at a distance of four hundred yards. That was almost the peak accuracy of the weapon. Allen didn't know the other trainees, but they didn't look like common drifters.

About the third week in camp, Allen realized that professional men were here, too—lawyers, doctors, policemen, as well as white-collar managers. Most were here to sharpen their skills, but Allen began to see the power and reach of the Sheppards. It amazed Allen that the trainees didn't talk to each other while training.

These were men who hadn't attended the meetings Allen had gone to, so it didn't bother him not to speak. The only thing that kept gnawing at Allen was why Balkner wanted him to murder Roger Singleton.

Even though Allen was a bit amused at the paramilitary training, he was ready to go home. Living in this area near the mountains was getting old. Even though he had been in Seattle for some time, he had never ventured this far out of the city.

Allen had several messages on his answering machine when he got home. The Sheppards had provided him with a driver Allen didn't know, so there wasn't much to talk about on the trip back to Seattle. He was exhausted after spending weeks at the camp, but he wanted to talk to Casey. He dialed Casey's number and waited until her answering machine came on. He left a message for Casey to call him. Then he called Leo Simon.

"Hello, Mr. Simon, this is Allen Wilson. How are you?"

"I'm fine, Allen. How was training?"

"It went well. The reason I called was to get an update from you."

Leo got a little antsy at that. He knew Allen was a bright young man and he couldn't pull the wool over his eyes forever. "I have to level with you. Eugene didn't trust you. He's a very smart man, and he wanted to be sure that you weren't some plant, trying to infiltrate our organization."

Allen answered quickly, "What do you think, Leo?"

"Look, Allen, we've never asked you about your education or background. And I think that's because Eugene wanted to use you."

"So why are you telling me this now?"

"Because you can handle it. You've passed a crucial test. Expect a visit from Balkner soon."

"I will."

Eugene meant well, Leo thought, but the idea of killing someone as a personal vendetta sort of shook Leo up. "Why don't you get some rest, Allen, and I'll be in touch."

"Sure, Leo. And thanks for the advice."

"Just keep it between us."

Allen hung up the phone smiling, thinking he had a leg up on Eugene Balkner.

Eugene was informed that Allen Wilson had completed his training. Now he would put Allen to the test. The flight from Philadelphia went well, and the cab ride from the airport to the hotel was memorable. Eugene had gotten the cab even though two Japanese tourists had wanted it. Eugene had flashed his Sheppard ring to the cabbie, and the cabbie then rushed past the Japanese tourists and put Eugene's baggage in his trunk. Eugene would be meeting Allen at Leo's home. There they would discuss Roger.

"Hello, Eugene. How was the trip?"

"Fine, Leo. Thanks for asking." Both men went inside Leo's modest home by the bay. "How's Wilson?"

"He's taking to it well, Eugene. He's a very strong man."

"Good. Now we can see what he's made of."

"What do you plan to do?" Eugene had to put Wilson to the test. He wanted to get Allen Wilson dirty, so he couldn't turn on the Sheppards in any court of law. Eugene couldn't be sure, but Casey could be deceptive. Eugene would trap Allen in a spider web he couldn't get out of. Eugene couldn't tell

Leo about his suspicion that Casey being behind Allen's sudden appearance. "Listen, Leo, I want to get things started with Allen Wilson right away."

"Good. I'll call him."

Leo reached Allen, and the younger man said he'd be right over. Leo was single, so he never worried about someone eavesdropping.

Allen arrived at Leo's home thirty minutes later. He was curious about what was going to take place. When he knocked on the door and Leo opened it, Allen was surprised to see Eugene there, but he remembered Leo's words. "Hello, Mr. Balkner, Good to see you," Allen said as genuinely as possible, trying to stay relaxed as he shook Eugene's hand.

"Allen, it's good to see you, too," Eugene said. "Now let's get down to business, gentlemen. By now you know what I want you to do. I want results and I think you can give them to me."

"Well, Eugene, I see you're a driven man."

"I'd be lost without ambition," Eugene replied somberly.

Leo brought some refreshments. "Soda, anyone?"

"Sure, I'll take one, Leo." Eugene was feeling thirsty from the trip. A soda would do him some good. Allen refused. Eugene took several gulps of the 7-Up and then put the can down.

He turned his attention back to Allen. "Allen, you know what I want. And it isn't because I hate Roger Singleton. No. It's a matter of principle." Then Eugene suddenly shouted, "Because I can't have this!" as he rammed his fist on the coffee table.

"Easy, Eugene," Leo said, trying to calm his friend.

"Well, dammit, Leo, I've tried to handle this diplomatically, but that foolhearted daughter of mine leaves me no choice."

"Think about it, Eugene." Leo wanted to buy Allen some time, but Eugene would have none of it.

"I have thought about this long and hard, Leo!" Then Eugene gave Leo an intimidating stare and Leo wilted under the pressure.

Eugene went on, "Allen, I've arranged for you to eliminate Roger Singleton. I know this is asking a lot, but I'm sure you feel the way I do." Eugene waited for a reply. Allen said nothing. "You might be a bit nervous now, but once you get started, it'll be a piece of cake."

Allen realized that he was dealing with a very sick man. Eugene had distorted his view of what was right so much that he'd forgotten all about the basic rights of others. Allen had to go along with this twisted plot. "Okay, Eugene, what's the plan?" Allen forced himself to say.

"Good, Allen. I'm going to send two Sheppards with you to help you complete the assignment. They are my eyes and ears on this assignment. Plus that will make it easier for you." Allen smiled at Eugene, a sort of uneasy smile that didn't sit well with Casey's father. "Everything's okay, isn't it?"

"No, it's not okay. I'm still trying to get used to this idea. I'm putting my life on the line here."

"Wait a minute. If it's the police you're worried about, I understand. But we have to take that chance."

Allen caught himself before answering. A smart reply wouldn't help matters. "By the way, Eugene, who are these two men?"

"They're two of my handpicked men—Mel Rose and Kent Gardener." Eugene knew that these two had a bone to pick with Roger because of a scuffle they had gotten into several months ago. These men wanted revenge, but he wanted them mainly to hound dog Allen.

Allen, on the other hand, was ready to go along with the plot, but he couldn't quell his nagging conscience. Conscience or not, he also had to keep his identity hidden.

"So when's the big day, Eugene?" Allen was looking pensively at Casey's father.

"In two weeks, Allen. I'll have Leo call you and tell you where to go."

Eugene eyed his protégé. Allen said nothing. Eugene went on, "we'll have everything you need."

As Allen prepared to leave, both Eugene and Leo stood up. "We'll be with you in spirit, son. God bless you!"

Allen almost let out a sigh as he left Leo's home. The nerve of him, Allen said to himself as he headed for his car.

Mel Rose and Kent Gardener were both hard cases. Mel had served several years in prison for assault with a deadly weapon, and Kent was a hothead from Spokane who would kill or maim anything just for sport. Eugene had run into these two about a year ago. They appeared to be naturals as disciples of the Sheppards. Eugene instantly liked their attitude. He had shown the men a picture of Roger that he'd swiped from Casey's apartment. They never forgot it. When Eugene heard about the little skirmish the men had had with Roger, he knew he could use them. He didn't want Kyle Mitchell or Tim Sanders: They were wet behind the ears—too soft for Eugene's taste. He wanted hard-core killers for this job.

As he stood up to leave, he took one last look around—a simple home, but effective. "I'll be in touch, Leo."

"Certainly, chief." Leo watched as Eugene walked out. That man is an explosion waiting to happen, he thought. He was concerned about Allen's life.

Eugene had a secret, which Leo suspected. If Allen faltered or turned coward when it came to killing Roger, Eugene would have the two men kill him.

Allen knew he was into something very dangerous. He didn't feel good about this arrangement, especially the two people going with him. On the way back to his apartment, he decided to get in touch with his brother William. When he arrived home, he checked his answering machine and then faxed his brother. Allen was taking no chances. In his fax, he explained to William what was going on in Seattle. When Allen received William's faxed reply, he was shocked. William explained to Allen that the two men were there to make sure the job was done either way. Allen could end up dead. Allen winced at the sharp advice from his brother. There was something gnawing at my gut, Allen thought to himself as he read the fax.

After shredding the fax reply, Allen decided to call Casey. He couldn't tell her everything; that would tear the whole case apart. Allen could go to the police, yet that would spell suicide. Eugene would stop at nothing. As Allen contemplated his next move, Leo called. "Allen Wilson speaking." It was Leo on his caller ID.

"Hello, Allen. It's Leo. I wanted to tell you to watch yourself. I don't know what Eugene is up to. He's very secretive about things. He may have paid those two men to finish the job if things were too much for you, so I'd watch my back if I were you."

Allen thought that he could trust Leo, at least a little, so he asked him, "What do you get out of this?"

Leo stammered a bit before saying, "I only want to live in peace. Now Eugene has a twisted view of "Leo cut himself short. "Just be careful, Allen." Then Leo hung up.

Allen thought about Leo's words— "Be careful, Allen." They resonated down to his bones. Allen had to let Casey know how far things had progressed. He decided to write her a letter. Allen sang, "Sarah Smile" by Harlan Oates, as he began the letter on his kitchen table.

Eugene checked into the Regency Hotel. Mel had Kyle Mitchell and Tim Sanders watching Casey's apartment, just in case. Eugene had a gut feeling about Allen Wilson. He's just too savvy to be a drifter, Eugene thought over and over again. Allen seemed to be a well-educated man. Eugene knew he couldn't take any chances. He had too much at stake.

I was at Casey's, getting ready for Chu to come and pick me up for work. The March weather was still cool at night, and it still rained regularly, yet I liked this time of year. Chu and I would clean several offices and then make the drug deliveries. Doing business with Chu brought in at least $2,000 a week. I gave Casey $500 weekly, and I kept a couple hundred a week. The rest I put in my stash in my car at home.

Dad was always glad to see me. We spoke freely about my mother returning home from Utah. Daisy and Pal were still dating, and I would always tease Daisy about her love life.

Chu drove up to the complex and blew his horn three times in quick succession. This was our signal. This was Wednesday night, so Chu and I would be making a pickup in the red-light district. I was a bit nervous as I went out into the van. "Hello, my man, Chu. How are you?"

"Couldn't be better, my man!"

"Good, let's go to it!"

"Alright." We buckled up and headed out. We had no idea that the two men down the street in the green Nova were keeping an eye on the apartment.

"Hey, Kent, what do you say we knock on the door and see if the nigger-loving bitch will open it—what do you say?" Mel screeched, almost foaming at the mouth. Kent sat up in his seat and put the beer can down.

"Mel, do you think that I'm going to mess with Eugene Balkner's daughter?! Hell, no.

Look at that poor nigger Roger!"

Both men chuckled at the thought of the overprotective father, yet Mel got the point. "Yeah, all we need is Balkner hiring someone to shoot us!"

"Right," Kent replied. They were watching Casey's apartment to see who came by, especially anybody involved with the Sheppards. "I'm feeling a little frisky, though," Mel said, anxious to go and hassle a few ladies for sex. Both men were heavy drinkers for people in their twenties.

Mel worked at Joe's Boat Repair as a clerk, and Kent Gardener was unemployed. The two men usually paid for cheap sex whenever they could get it. Tonight was no different than any other, and they wanted some. After two hours sitting on Casey's apartment, Mel spoke first. "Let's get out of here, Kent. No one's coming—I'm sure of it!"

"What time is it?"

"It's 8:30."

"Yeah, let's beat it." Then, just as Mel was about to start the beat-up green '86 Nova, a Seattle Police car pulled up behind them. "Oh, shit," Mel said nervously. He didn't bother to start the engine. Seconds later a tap on the window forced Mel to roll it down. "What are you fellas doing here?" the police officer said, as he prepared to ask them for some identification.

"Well, officer, we're just sitting here talking. That's all," Mel said.

"Where do you gentlemen live?" Stumped, Mel sat there dumbfounded. He was sure that he'd be hauled in because the officer smelled alcohol on his breath. "Eugene Balkner sends his love." The policeman tapped on the car with his nightstick and walked away.

Mel and Kent were both dumbstruck. "I don't believe it!" Mel kept saying to himself. Kent felt so relieved he wanted to release his bowels. "Mel, as soon as the cop pulls away you think we can leave?"

"Why wait," Mel said confidently. He then cranked up the old, but smooth-running vehicle and the pair drove off.

Officer Lynn Summers watched the pair drive off. He knew that they had been drinking, but Summers was a fellow Sheppard and had a few himself sometimes. He thought long and hard about Eugene's plan. Summers wouldn't stop the hit, but if he were forced to play his hand, he'd have to turn Eugene in. Summers shuddered as he observed the apartments. He knew that Allen Wilson wasn't who he said he was, yet Summers didn't know that Allen was playing both sides of the fence. For right now he'd keep an eye on the apartment, and then he'd make his normal rounds. A big man, Summers weighed well over two hundred pounds. His penetrating blue eyes and muscular physique gave the impression that the officer was a model. As a young kid, that had been his goal, but the orgies and travel quickly soured Summers on the modeling life. He blew a kiss to Casey's complex as he drove away.

Allen

CHAPTER 10

THE HIT

Eugene had set everything up. It was almost two weeks since he had spoken to Allen Wilson. That Monday night, Eugene had brought the rifle over to Leo's home. Mel Rose and Kent Gardener were there. Eugene had an infrared scope on the M16 rifle, and he was sure that with the training Allen had received he would be successful. If not, then Mel would take care of Allen with the nine millimeter he'd have in his waistband.

Allen arrived at Leo's at 2 a.m.

"Come on in, Allen," Leo said.

Allen had a hundred thoughts racing through his mind at once. A well-composed man, he had to stay calm. When they started driving over, he'd figure out what to do. He'd try to shoot Roger in the leg. Hopefully, Roger would drop and the three of them would hightail it out of there. Allen wouldn't check to see if Roger were dead or not. At this point that's the best he could ask for. He'd have completed the assignment. Then Eugene would have to get somebody else.

"Ready, Allen?" Eugene said, as he patted Allen on the back like a good friend.

"I'm ready," Allen said calmly, looking directly at Eugene. Eugene held the stare. Allen could see the wild intelligence in Eugene's eyes.

Eugene brought out the weapon. Leo checked through the window to make sure no one was outside. Leo knew the Sheppards had a dozen or so members who were policemen. They were mostly foot-patrol officers; the higher-ups didn't want to risk their careers on a questionable affiliation.

Several were Masons, too, but as far as he knew they were legitimate policemen. The officers who were Sheppards had to keep their affiliation low profile.

Eugene began giving instructions. "Now, look, Allen. We've been watching Roger, and we have it all worked out. When his buddy drops him off at around 4 in the morning, we'll have him."

"Who's his buddy?" Allen asked nonchalantly.

"He's a Chinaman," Eugene said. "But we don't want him. I want as little trouble as possible. I want Singleton!"

"Sure," Allen replied. He put up as little fuss as possible—that seemed like the wisest course.

"Okay, Allen. Mel and Kent are going to drive you to a location several hundred feet from Casey's apartment. You'll sit in the back seat and set your sights on Singleton. It should be very simple."

"Yeah!" Mel yelled.

Eugene patted Mel on the back. "Easy, Mel. We'll do this soon enough!"

Mel couldn't wait. He knew that if Allen failed to carry out the assignment, his job was to take him to a desolate location and kill him.

Eugene handed Allen the weapon. Allen slowly put the silencer on the rifle that was loaded with four rounds, and wrapped the rifle in a thin blanket.

Allen, Mel, and Kent then headed outside to an '89 white Ford van, one Eugene had bought just for this job. Mel had a pint of Seagram's Seven. He broke the seal, twisted the cap off, and took a hard swig. "Damn! Want a buck snort, Wilson?"

"No, I work better sober. Let's get moving."

"In time, Wilson. We still have a couple hours to kill." Mel took another hard swig.

"Let me have some of that, Mel," Kent said. Mel passed Kent the bottle. Kent puckered up and took three good swigs. The bottle was half-empty now, and Kent screwed the top back on.

"Sure you're okay, Wilson?" Kent shoved the bottle in Allen's direction.

"No, thanks, gentlemen."

Kent put the bottle under the seat. "Have it your way, Wilson."

Mel checked the time. It was quarter to three. "Let's head out," Mel said anxiously. The men all prepared for the ride over. On the way, Mel turned on some heavy metal. "Hey! Keep that down," Allen said sharply.

"I'll turn it down soon enough. Don't worry, Wilson." Mel got a kick out of aggravating Allen Wilson. Exasperated, Allen tried to concentrate despite the noise. He knew he had to make it look good. He hoped his letter had reached Casey.

Casey had read Allen's letter with grave concern. Allen had told her some details about the hit on Roger. The PI said that Eugene was going through with the hit, but Allen didn't know when. He wouldn't know until the night Eugene called him, so Allen was warning Casey as best he could. Casey knew that Allen was in a tough situation. She realized, too, that she couldn't tell Roger what she knew, even though keeping it to herself was tearing her apart. Roger would have to get by on his own wits now.

It was an easy night tonight, so at 3:30 a.m. Chu decided to call it a night. "What do you say Roger—you ready to get some sleep?" Chu asked.

"Sure, Chu, I'm kind of beat."

"Okay, I'll swing by your apartment." Chu and I had cleaned half our usual accounts. Then we'd made our drug deliveries. Tonight's take was well over $3,000. Chu gave me $1,000. "This will keep you smiling for a few days, my man."

"Thanks, Chu. I can really use it."

"I know the feeling," Chu said as he glanced over at me. Chu knew what it was like to have to scrape and scrap for everything. Now he was a wealthy man, yet if he were ever caught, he could lose everything. Chu had done all he could to make money legitimately. For the rest he circulated easily in the underworld. He noticed that I never talked about my boss, Mr. Gillione. That was just fine with Chu. He didn't like a lot of questions about his business.

However, Chu liked me; he didn't mind doing business with this cool black man. Chu just wished that I had more friends. I was a loner, and that bothered Chu. "Here, we go, Roger, right in front of your place. Take it easy on Casey, eh?"

"I sure will, Chu. And thanks, man, for everything." We shook hands, and I got out of Chu's van and headed for Casey's apartment.

Mel had situated the white Ford van so that as soon as Allen took the shots, they could speed away without making a U-turn.

Kent had the night-vision binoculars. "Hey, here comes the nigger, Wilson. Quick—get ready," Kent said.

Allen had been sitting in the back seat of the van with the sliding door opened. As I headed for the door, Allen got me in his sights. Allen knew he could have killed me, but that's not what he wanted to do. I got to the door and went for my keys. Casey's apartment door faced the street, which gave Allen a clear shot. Allen got off three shots in a quick burst, and I went down.

"You got him," Kent whispered, very excited. "Let's get out of here!"

Mel quickly pulled the van onto the street and sped away.

I heard the van start up and screech away. I had screamed when I was hit. My left thigh was burning horribly and blood was oozing onto the steps. I could hear the hissing sound as the bullets slammed into adjoining buildings. I stayed down and pulled out my thirty-eight. I had to get to Casey. I took out my cell phone. Then I changed my mind: Instead of waking up Casey, I called 911.

Mel got Allen over to Leo's as fast as possible. They gave Leo the weapon. Then Allen left without saying a word. He drove to his apartment, got out, went inside, and packed a suitcase. Allen figured he'd lay low for a while and then sneak back and get the rest of his things. Bag packed, he went out to his Toyota pickup, threw the suitcase in the back, and took off. He was heading to Cleveland.

Leo called Eugene with the news. "They pulled it off. Now what?"

"Just take it easy, Leo. Let's see what happens."

"Well, Allen left the weapon with me, and Mel and Kent said that he hit Singleton and that Singleton went down. They didn't hang around to see if he was dead."

"Let's wait and see." Eugene didn't like this situation. If Singleton survived, then the plan he had so carefully devised would all be for naught.

"Keep the weapon hidden, Leo, and I'll get back to you."

"Sure thing, boss!" Leo put down the receiver. He wondered what Eugene would do next.

Anne knew why Eugene was going back to Seattle. He wouldn't let it go. He was the one making trouble for Casey. They had a big argument about it. It got so violent that Eugene hit Anne several times—hard enough to draw blood. Anne told Eugene that if went to Seattle, she'd leave him. Eugene just brushed the comment aside and headed out. He'd packed his suitcases earlier, so all he had to do was call a cab and leave.

Anne couldn't believe it! She feared for her life, so she wouldn't go to the authorities, but she could go live somewhere else. She thought of Casey, and then Anne began packing. She had $4,000 stashed away. Eugene rarely gave her more than enough money to pay the bills and take care of household needs. She had managed to save the money through years of penny pinching.

I lay in a hospital bed. The authorities had awakened Casey and gotten her to answer the door. When they explained to her that I had been shot, she fainted. When she regained consciousness, she found out that I had been hit in the back of the upper thigh. The bullet had ripped through muscle and sinew and had left a gaping hole in the back of my leg. The bullet had gone straight through. Despite the injury, doctors said I was a lucky man. The surgeon cleaned the wound and tried to sew some remaining muscle tissue together.

I had lost a lot of blood, but I never blacked out. "Hey, doctor, how does it look?" I asked in slight pain. The morphine was making me woozy.

"Son, it looks horrible, but it will heal. You'll have to take it easy for a while."

I knew that Eugene was behind the shooting, but when the police arrived, my mind went blank.

Hank Albright entered the room to question me. He recognized me from his investigation of the Gillione murders. "Hello, Roger. Looks like you had some trouble. Care to tell me anything?" Albright was being careful; he knew not to move too fast.

"Officer?"

"Detective Hank Albright. We've met."

"Oh yeah, when Mr. Gillione was killed." I was a bit out of it from the drugs, but I still kept my composure. Being too talkative could spell trouble.

"What can you tell me, Roger? Did you see the shooter?"

"I heard shots, and then I was hit. I remember falling to the ground, and then I heard tires screeching away."

"So, you don't know why anyone would want to kill you, Roger?" Albright was feeling out the situation. Maybe the guys who'd killed Gillione were gunning for Singleton, too.

"Anything you want to tell me? Anything at all?"

"Yeah, officer. Find whoever did this." I was careful. I had to play my cards close to the vest. People like Balkner could strike anywhere, but mainly I was worried about my family. And God forbid I tell this detective what Chu had confided in me.

Hank studied me. The sedatives were working, so he thought he'd come back later. "Okay Roger, get some rest. We'll talk another time, okay?"

"Hey, officer, when you find them, tell them to go. . ." I dozed off. Hank figured I was stoned on the morphine, so he left my room.

Officer Lynn Summers had heard about the shooting. He also heard that Roger was still alive. *I wonder how Mr. Balkner will take that*, Summers thought. He knew part of what happened, but his loyalty to the Sheppards took precedence right now. Officer Summers could have blown the case wide open, yet he chose to remain silent.

Casey was furious at Allen Wilson. She questioned his sincerity and his integrity. *I gave him so much money. How could he let this happen?* she kept asking herself. Casey was very close to going to the authorities, but she knew her father would strike out against anyone he could, especially Roger's family. For now Casey planned on staying silent, yet she still had trouble believing what Allen Wilson had done.

Eugene got a call from Lynn Summers. Roger was still alive. Eugene was livid. "Damn that Allen Wilson! He's either a lousy shot or he. . ." Eugene let the words trail off. *He deliberately missed! That's it. Allen must have planned the whole thing.* Eugene knew that a leg shot had to be aimed well and pure. He called Leo. "Leo, this is Eugene. Where's Allen?"

"As far as I know, he's at his apartment."

"Well get hold of him, and have him call me."

"Sure, Eugene. I'll be in touch." Leo hung up. Allen surely wasn't at his apartment, but Leo decided he'd call there anyway.

A week passed. I was released from the hospital. "Casey, where's my cell phone, girl?"

"It's in the car."

"What's it doing in the car? Damn!"

"Sorry, honey. I used it yesterday."

"I'll get it," I said angrily. I got my crutches and went outside to fetch my cell phone. After the shooting, I always carried my thirty-eight. I would fight first now. Madeline had called to say that there was an opening at her job at the pier; I declined. Working with Chu was just fine for me.

I got the cell phone and hopped back into the apartment. There were three messages on the phone, and I checked them.

One was from Chu. "Hey, Roger, get in touch with me."

The second was from Hank Albright. The third message was from Mom. "Hello, Roger, I'm out of rehab, and I have an apartment here in Utah. I'm searching for my family. I found one of my sisters and we're having a ball. Call me." I knew Mom would make it now; she was finding her roots. I'd get in touch with her, but I had to call dad and let him know I was okay. "Hey, Roger," Casey said. "You want to go to a movie tonight?"

"Well, my leg is sore. How about when it feels better?"

"Okay, I understand. Well, I'm going to work; I'll see you this evening. Give me a kiss. Love you."

"Alright, babe. Be careful!"

"I will." Casey left the apartment.

I contemplated my next move, and decided to call my father. I got the answering machine. "Hello, Dad. It's Roger. Give me a call when you can."

Anne was living in a hotel in Spokane. She had been there for several days. She didn't want to make trouble for Casey, but she had to get away from Eugene. Anne had pondered over whether or not to call; she decided to call the apartment. I picked it up after a few rings.

"Hello."

"Hello, Roger, this is Anne Balkner."

"How are you, Mrs. Balkner?"

"I'm fine, Roger. How about you?"

"I'm doing well. I'm recovering. Thanks."

"Oh, I'm sorry. I didn't know you were sick!"

"I was shot."

"Oh, God!" Anne became quiet.

"You okay, Mrs. Balkner?"

Anne composed herself, then said, "Yes, I'm fine. Do you know who's responsible for the shooting, Roger?"

"No, not yet. The police are working on it." Anne knew, but she decided to play it cool. "I hope they find whoever is responsible."

"Me, too, Mrs. Balkner."

"By the way, Roger, I'm in Spokane, and I was wondering—could I come over for a visit?"

"Sure, Mrs. Balkner, but I'll have to get Casey to come pick you up."

"Okay, Roger. And thanks. By the way, I'm at Motel Six in Spokane off the interstate going west."

"I'll be sure and tell Casey, Mrs. Balkner."

"I'll be expecting her. Have her call me." Anne gave Roger the number and then hung up. She was furious. Eugene was a sick man. Anne didn't think a psychiatrist could help him, but someone had to. Anne began crying to herself. She felt for Casey.

Allen had arrived in Cleveland and immediately wrote Casey a letter. He explained to her what he had had to do. That he had saved Roger's life and possibly put his own at risk. He had to leave town, and he'd be in Cleveland for a while. Allen sent Casey back $10,000. He figured that was the least he could do.

When Leo didn't hear back from Allen, he told Eugene. This aroused Eugene's suspicion. Eugene wondered what Allen's intentions were. He realized that Allen had enough information about him to go to the authorities. Eugene had friends in high places, but if things got out of hand, those friends would leave him out in the cold. He pondered his next move. Finding Allen Wilson was his top priority.

Casey had gotten the message from me. She was thrilled that her mother was in Washington State. Casey left work early to pick her up. Anne had spoken briefly to Casey over the phone and now the two were going to meet. Casey didn't mind the drive over to Spokane. Once she arrived at the motel, she immediately went to her mother's room. Upon seeing each other, the two of them embraced. Anne couldn't stop crying.

"I am so sorry, darling. I heard about Roger."

"Oh, Mom. I didn't mean to bring you into this!"

"Your father and I had an argument, and I decided to leave. It's not your fault." Both women looked long and hard at each other and both understood without saying a word what they were dealing with. "Casey, I hope you realize that your father is behind this."

"I know, Mom, but he's still my father."

"Yes, dear." Casey walked her mother to the car. When they arrived in Seattle and got to Casey's apartment, Anne was exhausted. "Casey, if you don't mind, I just want to get in bed and get some rest."

"Sure, Mom." When they went inside, Anne gave me a hug and went straight to the guest room. Casey managed to get her luggage inside and then locked the door. "I hope you don't mind, Roger."

"Not at all, Casey, not at all."

The next day I still hadn't heard from my dad. I decided to call my mother.

Charlotte wanted to talk to me. "Hello, Roger. I'm glad to hear from you. I miss you."

"Miss you, too, Mom. How are you?"

"I'm fine. Look, I've found most of my family. It feels good to be clean, son; I haven't felt this good in a long time."

"I'm happy for you, Mom. When are you coming back to visit?"

"I don't know. I'm enjoying myself here in Utah."

"Aw, Mom. Come and visit. I'll be waiting for you.

"I'll think about it, Roger."

"Well, Mom, I'll be in touch. Love you."

"Love you, too, Roger." I was happy that my mother was putting her life back together. I hope Mom doesn't lose her sobriety; she's worked hard for this, I thought. I decided to get some rest, since I was there alone. Anne had gone with Casey to Casey's job for the day. I cherished my solitude now that I was injured. It meant that I didn't have to do much running around the apartment. I could rest my sore leg.

Casey

CHAPTER 11

PHILLY

Casey received Allen's letter. It was almost two weeks since I had been shot, and the wound was healing nicely. I was getting around without crutches. I still had to limp around, and Casey had to check the wound from time to time, but I was definitely getting better. Allen had explained to Casey some details of Eugene's plot. Casey was somewhat relieved when she saw the check for $10,000. It earned him back some of her respect.

Anne had planned to live with Casey and me until Eugene stopped his madness or confessed to the authorities. Chances were slim, but at least it was worth a try. Anne had left messages for Eugene several times and told him where she was. She told Eugene in one message that she would speak to him only with Casey and Roger present. Anne also told Eugene that she hoped he didn't have anything to hide. She patiently waited for Eugene's reply.

Allen had called a Seattle-based furniture moving company, as well as his landlord, and had had all his belongings loaded and shipped to Cleveland. Allen didn't plan to go back to Seattle. Eugene Balkner had Allen in his sights, and Allen wanted to steer clear of him. Allen planned to stay in touch with Casey, but he was definitely considering another line of work.

Eugene called Anne. He tried to sound as contrite as possible, but he suspected that both Anne and Casey were aware of his plan. "Hello, Anne. I've been thinking. Why don't you, Casey, and I get together for lunch the next time I'm in Seattle?" Eugene asked.

Anne was still very skeptical of Eugene. His racist attitude was something Anne had began to despise. Having someone shoot such a nice young man like Roger—that had really hurt Anne. She wasn't sure if she wanted to patch things up. "I'll have to think about that, Eugene, okay? I mean I'm still upset at you for hitting me. That's not like you."

"Oh, Anne, I lost my head, that's all. I promise it won't happen again."

"We'll see." Eugene pressed the issues. His chances were slim, but he could use her to find out some things. "Anne, I want you and Casey to meet me here in Philadelphia at our apartment."

"Only if Roger comes with us."

Eugene's blood pressure spiked. He hadn't planned on that. Eugene knew he had to pretend he had no problem with the suggestion. "Okay, Anne, that'll be fine."

"Good, we'll be there in two days."

"Good-bye, Anne."

"Good-bye." Anne put the phone down, thinking that she might finally get to the bottom of things. Anne presented Casey with the idea.

"I'm not sure, Mom. Roger may not like the idea of seeing Dad."

"He's got to see him, Casey. That way he could identify Eugene if he had to."

Casey thought about that. A meeting would give Roger the advantage. Eugene couldn't do anything directly because Roger would know what he looked like. "I'll run it by Roger and see what he says."

"Sure, dear." Both women then relaxed, hoping to catch a good program on television.

I had finally gotten in touch with my dad. Dad had heard about my injury from Madeline. He knew I was very fortunate. I could have easily lost my life. Dad now knew why I had moved—it was to protect him and the girls.

We embraced upon seeing each other. Still limping a bit, I was feeling much better. I told Dad about Mom completing her rehabilitation program.

He was thrilled. "That's wonderful news, son. When is she coming back to Seattle?"

"I'm not sure, Dad. Mom seems to have found her family, and she wants to stay in Utah for a while." He let my statement sink in. His life had touched him. He wanted to spend time with her again. "I'll be glad to see Charlotte, son."

"I know you will, Dad." I liked where things were heading. It would be great for my mother and father to get back together.

"Tell me something, son. Your boss who was killed—what really happened?"

"I'm in the dark about Mr. Gillione. I'm just sorry he's dead."

"You know, with you getting shot and all, do you think it's safe living with that white woman?"

"Well, Dad, I know that death is a part life—and I have to accept that."

"It's nice to see that you have matured, son, but premature death is still a hard pill to swallow."

"I think I'll be alright, Dad. Just have to play my cards right, that's all."

"Just be careful, son."

"I will, dad." I then excused myself and went to lie down in my room for a while. My leg had stiffened up.

When I arrived at Casey's apartment, Casey was waiting for me.

"Hello, Roger. Everything okay?"

"So far, sweetheart." I limped toward her and gave her a kiss.

"Roger, I have to talk to you about something."

"What is it, babe? Is it something serious?"

"It's very serious Roger; I want you to fly back to Philadelphia with Mom and me to see my father." I tried to comprehend what Casey was saying, and why. I knew that Eugene wanted me dead, and to go to the man's home—it was unthinkable! "Look, Casey," I said, trying to keep my cool, "I know you mean well, but that would be suicide!"

"No, I don't think so. You see, Dad can't just do away with Mom and me. So as long as you're with us, you should be okay."

"I just don't know, Casey. Your father has his own take on things."

"Roger, we're trying to get you to see Dad face to face. Then he can't do anything to you himself because you'd recognize him." Casey looked at me pleadingly.

I felt trapped. If I refused to go to Philly, it would mean either a fight or a separation. "OK. I'll go with you to visit your dad, but I'll be on my guard."

"Thanks, Roger. By the way, did you know that Allen is off the case?"

"He is?" Shocked, I still managed to keep my cool. "Damn! I'd have never thought it. Why?"

"I think he knows who shot you and now he's running for his life." I whistled, amazed at this turn of events.

"I wouldn't be surprised. Your father is some twisted mutha," I exclaimed.

"Well, Mom and I are going to get our things ready for the trip. Are you scared, too?" Casey started laughing, but she gave me a big hug, letting me know it was all in fun.

"Okay, Casey. So you think your dad has people running to all parts of the globe to get away from him?" I had to laugh at that one myself, just as Anne came into the room.

"What's so funny, you two? Have you been looking at Eugene's picture again?"

"Ha-ha. No, Mom, we're just having a laugh at Dad's expense—that's all."

Anne became upset. She didn't see anything funny about it, especially after my incident. "Well, Casey, your father isn't a man who likes to be mocked—understand that, dear!"

"Yes, Mother."

Anne was aware of Eugene's hair-trigger temper: He could fly off the handle, possibly attacking all three of them, if provoked. He'd lost the element of surprise, so now he might be desperate. She needed Casey to understand this and act respectful toward Eugene while in his presence. Anne felt compelled to warn Casey and me. "Look, you two, we are dealing with a man who is used to getting his way. Eugene will stop at nothing. He'd just as soon do away with us as kill a bug on a windshield without remorse. I'm telling you this because I love you both." Tears streaming down her face, Anne motioned for the two of us to come over. The three of us embraced. I was trying to get a handle on this weird family dynamic. It would be a long trip.

As he washed the dishes, Eugene knew he had to be on his best behavior. If he reacted negatively toward Roger, he stood a chance not only of losing his wife and possibly killing Roger. He would then have to deal with the authorities who responded to the scene. He had to feel his way through things. He'd order the food and bottled water. He didn't want to arouse suspicion, even in trivial matters like these. I wonder, he thought. Can I hold my tongue in front of that nigger, Roger? He certainly has put a damper on my plans. I don't understand it. All the decent white men and Casey wants a black, Eugene wondered to himself. Then he remembered the stories of black men's sexual prowess. Eugene had heard that some black men's penises were at least thirteen inches long. Eugene tried to imagine an organ stretched thirteen inches. Boy, with that much blood flowing through it, it's a wonder the guy could stay conscious while he thrusted, never mind the poor woman. Eugene felt more than comfortable with his seven inches. It gave him versatility, and on more than one occasion he'd brought women to climax. Even though he and Anne hadn't screwed for over one year, he would still get quite excited fondling Anne and groping her. Anne loved it, but Eugene would go as far as manipulating her with his fingers to bring Anne to orgasm. He saved his penis for other women; he paid handsomely for their services.

Eugene composed himself. There had to be more to it than sex for Casey to want Singleton. They had to have some deeper connection. Maybe all my tirades about the incompetence of minorities made Casey curious, and her curiosity turned into desire. Whatever the reason, my dream of expanding the business to the West Coast—kaput. Eugene looked down. He was squeezing a plate so hard his knuckles had turned white. He put the dish down, and leaned against the refrigerator. He was starting to feel lightheaded, so he sat down at the kitchen table. One man might just have cost him millions. Eugene could never forgive his daughter; not only had she cost him a great deal of money, but she'd tried to bring shame upon his family's honor.

As a Sheppard, Eugene adhered to an unwritten code not to mix with "mud people." Now an occasional dip into a black vagina was okay, but no serious relationships. The Aryan race was already strained to the point of becoming degenerates, and marrying and copulating with those other than the superior race was just unacceptable. "Dammit!" Eugene said as he slammed his fist against the refrigerator. This meeting with Anne and that nigger-loving Casey with that black son-of-a-bitch Roger would be Eugene's biggest test yet. For now, Eugene had to lie down.

Casey had bought the plane tickets. I gave the Philadelphia address to my father and told him that if he didn't hear from him by Sunday to file a missing persons report. Dad wished me well and said, "I'll pray for you." I cried as I left my father and sisters.

The flight went smoothly. All three of us sat in the same row. I was able to stretch my legs out and sleep. Casey had given me a sedative. To her surprise this was my first flight.

Once we arrived in Philadelphia, Casey took over. "Okay, Mom and Roger, stay close. We'll get to Dad's place in no time."

"Okay, dear, we're counting on you," I quipped.

"Why don't we rent a car, Casey? That way your dad can't hold us if we decide to leave."

"That's a good idea, Roger. Then we can tour the city."

"Sure," Anne added. "Let's do that."

The three of us found the rental car desk, and after half an hour of negotiating, we had a nice slightly worn Lincoln Towne car. It was roomy enough. We packed the three suitcases in the trunk and headed for Eugene's.

"Casey, I don't mind visiting, but there's no way I'm sleeping over at your father's," I said.

Casey thought about that for a moment. "I'm with you, Roger. What about you, Mom?" Undecided, Anne said, "I should stay, Casey. After all, he's my husband."

"Well, you do whatever you think is right, Mom." As she drove, Casey glanced at her mother. Anne was looking content, yet apprehensive. "You sure, Mom? You really want to stay there?"

"Yes, I'll stay. But if things get out of control, I'll call you, okay?"

"Okay, Mom."

We made it to Eugene's apartment in one piece. Casey drove erratically. Maybe that was how everyone drove in the City of Brotherly Love.

Eugene was waiting for us. Anne unlocked the door with her key and ushered both Casey and me into the apartment. I spotted Eugene Balkner.

"Eugene," Anne said, trying to get her husband to show some manners.

"Boy," Eugene said to me sarcastically.

This relaxed me; I knew where I stood now. I forced myself to say, "Sir." Then I looked right at Eugene. I saw the disgust on his face, and for the first time I had the feeling my dad said he got from certain whites. I began to feel uncomfortable, and Casey sensed it. She said, "Can we sit down, Dad?"

"Maybe, I don't want him rubbing black off on my chairs."

"Stop it, Eugene!" Anne cried. "Can't you behave for a few minutes! Roger was kind enough to travel here with us. The least you can do is show some respect!" Anne was outraged at Eugene, who noticed it and softened his stance.

"Well, Anne, I just don't know why Casey wants to date. . ." Eugene cut himself short.

"A black man, Dad?" Casey yelled. "You've always wanted to be in control. Now you want to control who I'm screwing!" Casey wanted to lash out at Eugene in response to his last remark.

"Casey!" Anne admonished her daughter. "Apologize immediately!"

Casey wasn't finished. "Mom, ever since Dad found out that Roger was black, he's been against me, and I'm sick of it!"

Everyone just stood there in the apartment hallway in angry silence. With a black man this close to his family, Eugene was ready to kill. At one point he was poised to kill the three of them and then turn the gun on himself. Only an eyelash of reasoning stopped him from doing that.

Anne was trying to keep her family together. She said, "Let's all just go in the living room and have a seat. We've had a long trip."

Looking menacingly at Roger, Eugene said, "I can stomach the boy now, so let's get down to business. I want you to come back, Anne!"

"I don't know, Eugene. You've changed into someone I can't trust anymore."

"Look, Anne, you've known how I've felt about these people for years. Why does it trouble you all of a sudden?"

"I just want you not to hate anymore, Eugene."

"Look, Anne, I don't want to lose what we have. We've come too far to let this happen."

"Eugene, you attacked me the other day. I can't forget that."

"Now, Anne, I can't begin to explain how I feel about you. We're family, for God's sake!"

"Oh, Eugene." Anne went over to Eugene and embraced him. "Tell me, did you have anything to do with Roger being shot?"

This caught Eugene off-guard, he didn't expect that. How did Anne figure that out? Eugene's worst fears had come to pass. However, he had to keep cool. "Anne, I'd never stoop to that level."

Anne knew Eugene was lying, but she decided to play along. "Okay, Eugene, I believe you."

Casey and Roger stood in the hallway in disbelief. They knew Eugene was a really twisted man.

Eugene then said, "Why don't I order takeout?"

Anne interrupted, "Casey, can you take me back to our room so I can get my bags? I'll stay here tonight."

Catching on to her mom's ploy, Casey went along. "Sure, Mom, let's go. Then we can pick up some food."

"Where are you staying, Anne? I can take you there."

"Oh, no, Eugene. You get the place ready, and we'll be right back."

"Well," Eugene shot back in a huff.

"Oh, come on, sweetheart." Anne went over and kissed Eugene.

"Okay, Anne. I'll straighten things up."

"We'll be back in a minute, Eugene."

Seconds later the three of us were in the Lincoln Towne car. Anne spoke first. "Let's drive back to Seattle, Casey. I'm afraid Eugene will come looking for us if we go to the airport." Casey checked the time; it was 7:30.

"Well, it's already dark, so I'm sure we'd have to wait at least an hour at the airport. Let's get some gas and hit the freeway," Anne said. She paused, and then added in a crushed voice, "That man was someone I used to admire. Now he's turned into an animal I can't bear to be with!"

"Yes, Mom," Casey said as she turned into the service station.

It was ten o'clock. Eugene couldn't believe he'd fallen for such a lame scheme. Casey must have had connections with Allen Wilson. Otherwise, how would she know? Now the authorities might get involved, and with Allen Wilson's knowledge of Eugene's role in the shooting, he stood a chance of being charged with attempted murder. Eugene felt like a trapped animal. He packed his suitcase and headed for the airport.

I wanted to call my father and tell him not to worry. It was the middle of the night in Seattle when I called, but Dad answered the phone. "Hello?"

"Hello, Dad. It's Roger. I'm fine, so don't worry about me. I'll be in touch. Now get some sleep."

"Talk to you later, son. Good-night." I hung up the phone, and hurried back to the car. We had stopped in Cleveland to rest for the night. We were searching for a motel. Casey had Allen's address, so she planned to call Directory Assistance to try to get Allen's phone number. We made it to a Motel Six.

"This will have to do, gang. We're on a tight budget," Anne said. "But anything beats living with Eugene. Thank God I didn't let you leave me there with him alone."

We decided to stay in one room. Famished, Casey ordered pizza. She then checked the local phone book and managed to find Allen Wilson's number through the return address on the letter he'd sent her. She'd call him in the morning. For now they all needed some rest.

At 7:30 the next morning, Casey called Allen.

"Hello?"

"Hello, Allen?"

"Yes?"

"This is Casey Balkner!"

"Casey, how did you get my number?"

"It was easy Allen. Now relax. I just wanted to let you know that we're passing through Cleveland, and I wanted to talk to you."

"Give me your address, and I'll be right over." Allen arrived an hour or so later, and was ushered in. I had taken a sedative and was still asleep. Anne, Casey, and Allen went outside. Casey spoke first after she embraced Allen. "So how's my private eye doing?"

"Ex-private eye, I'll have know."

"I just wanted to ask Allen: Would you go to the authorities if I asked you to?"

"Maybe; it depends. Why do you want to go to the authorities now?"

"I don't know. Maybe seeing for myself my dad's overwhelming arrogance. He thinks he can do anything he wants and get away with it. It sickens me!"

Anne decided it was her turn. "Now, I don't know you, young man, but if there's anything you want to tell us, please do."

"Allen Wilson, ma'am, and Eugene Balkner is one man that I want nothing to do with."

"You must really have been caught up in my husband's shenanigans."

"You're Mrs. Balkner? I figured you'd be as domineering as your husband."

"I'm ashamed of him now, Allen. And ashamed that I stayed with him this long." Anne lowered her head and turned to walk away.

"Mom, don't!" Casey said.

Allen realized that Eugene struck a chord of disgust in everyone he met.

When Anne went back into the motel room, Casey went over to Allen. The two embraced.

"Allen, I love Roger, and I thank you for not killing him."

"It's perfectly okay, Casey." Allen attempted to kiss Casey. She let him, and the two kissed long and hard. Casey broke away, "I need some room," Casey gasped.

"I feel it, too, Casey." They shook hands and Allen knew it was time to leave. "Good-bye, Casey,"

"Bye, Allen, and good luck!" Casey went back inside, feeling a bit guilty. Maybe she should have been with a white guy, but meeting Roger was something she couldn't get over. This easygoing black man with the charming personality had swept Casey off her feet. Casey and I had been together since that first meeting at the bank. Now she had feelings for Allen, too. Sometimes Casey didn't understand herself. She came over to me.

"Roger, wake up!" she said. I stirred, but I didn't quite awaken. "Okay, turn over so I can check your leg." Somehow I rolled over. Casey put some more salve on the wound. I jumped up but stayed asleep.

At around 9:30 a.m., I finally woke up. Anne and Casey had showered and dressed. They didn't discuss Allen, each for her own reasons. I got up, showered gingerly, and was ready to hit the road.

Anne, who had been deep in thought, said, "Roger, by now, Eugene's probably on a rampage. Call your family and tell them to leave home for a while. I don't want anything to happen to them."

That made sense. A bit woozy, I quickly dialed my father.

Eugene

CHAPTER 12

THE TORCHING

Eugene made it to Seattle two days after Anne had pulled her disappearing act. He was livid. He was also worried. He figured he'd really have to flex his muscles to show who was the boss. Casey and Anne had taken things too far, and all for that lousy nigger—it was just too much for Eugene. He called Leo Simon to pick him up at the airport. Leo got there as fast as he could.

Leo met Eugene at the terminal and said, "What brings you back to Seattle so soon?"

"They're onto me, Leo, and that damn Allen Wilson set me up. I'll kill him if I can get my hands on him!"

"Take it easy, Eugene!" Leo had never seen Eugene this worked up before. "Hey, let's go and have a drink at my place and think things out. What do you say?"

That sounded like a good idea. "Yeah, maybe that will calm me down, Leo."

The two men left the airport in Leo's pickup. Away from the crowds at the airport Leo asked Eugene, "How did you find out about Allen Wilson?"

"Through my wife. They knew I was the one behind that nigger's shooting!"

"I'll be damned," Leo bristled. "Then Allen must have been informing somebody about our activities."

"You got it, Leo!" Eugene barked.

"That son of a bitch!" Despite his outburst, Leo had to respect Allen Wilson's integrity. He certainly had balls to pull something like that off.

"Well, we'll show 'em who's boss!" Eugene snapped.

"Hold it!" Leo said. "We have to work together now. The policemen who are Sheppards are keeping us informed, but we can't make any stupid moves. We don't know how long they'll keep quiet."

"I have to move fast, or Casey and that nigger-loving wife of mine will go to the authorities!"

"Eugene, we'll just have to take that chance."

"Leo, just get me to a drink, alright?"

"Alright, boss!"

It was Saturday—a perfect night for a meeting, Eugene thought, as Leo drove to his house. He would call for an emergency meeting. They'd go to Casey's apartment first, and then he'd send someone to Roger's house. He'd get answers or else. "Hurry up, Leo, I'm ready to burst!" Leo said nothing as he sped home.

When they arrived at Leo's place and went inside, Eugene headed straight for the liquor cabinet. He grabbed the first thing he saw—the Scotch. Eugene took a hard, long drink. When he put the bottle down, he had to sit down and collect himself. Drinking on an empty stomach was dangerous, but drinking on a nervous stomach was self-destruction. Yet Eugene shook it off, saying, "Damn, that feels good. Get me Mel Rose, Leo—now!" Leo felt that something was driving Eugene, like a force that propelled only the demented. "I'll call him, Eugene. Now have another swig of that Scotch, and I'll be right back." Leo left Eugene and the bottle in the living room as he headed into the kitchen. I'll let him drink himself to sleep, and then I'll decide what to do, Leo thought. Leo was in this thing up to his neck; he still had the rifle used to shoot Roger tucked away in his bedroom. Any misstep, and they'd all be investigated. Leo then checked on Eugene; he had finished the Scotch, and now was in a drunken stupor. Good, Leo thought. Now maybe he'll calm down and stop ordering me around. Leo went into his bedroom and called the chairman. He told him to let everyone that there would be a meeting tonight.

Casey decided that they would take it slow driving back to Seattle. Anne and Casey talked intensely. Casey understood that, as a child, Eugene always got the short end of the stick. He had to work twice as hard as everyone else to get what he wanted. To Eugene, minorities were like rats after a piece of cheese. They would overrun America if they weren't kept in check. Casey was amazed that her mother had put up with Eugene's hatemongering for so long.

Anne's reply: "I heard Eugene's rhetoric for so l long that I even began to believe it." But every time she talked to a person of another race, she'd snap out of it.

I was fairly quiet. I was doing a lot of thinking. I hope Dad and the girls are okay. This shit is really getting me unnerved. I really could have hit Eugene for the way he was acting, but he's such a large man and my leg . . . I grimaced at the thought of trying to fight off Eugene. That would have been a real challenge. I planned my next move. I didn't want to call my father now. It might even be too late. They might have already packed and left home. There was nothing to do but enjoy the scenery.

For the meeting that night, Eugene had managed to pull himself together. A hot shower and several cups of strong, black coffee helped do the trick. The room was full. Through the grapevine, everyone had heard about Roger's shooting. All were eager to see what Eugene Balkner had up his sleeve.

Eugene took the podium. "Gentlemen, fellow Sheppards, I salute you. My brothers in Philadelphia send you their greetings. I know that I'm an outsider here in your territory, but, men, I've witnessed your dedication to this organization, and I'm impressed with your loyalty to each other."

Eugene had full command of the twenty or so members. "Look, men, by now you've all heard about my predicament and you know my feelings toward inferiors, but, men, we had a traitor among us—Allen Wilson!" This brought angry murmurs from the group. Eugene wanted to have as many people on his side as possible. "Now I want everyone's help in eliminating a problem that may compromise our organization."

The Sheppards remained silent. Finally, Leo spoke up. "I've got something to say, Eugene. Now, while we don't commit acts of violence ourselves, you are welcome to use some of our soldiers. But you're on your own."

"Wait, Leo!" Eugene tried in vain to override the backbone Leo had just displayed.

"No, you wait, Eugene. I think I speak for everyone here. You have stepped over the line. A personal dislike of someone doesn't warrant retaliation. Now if I had my way, I wouldn't back you. But since you're a well-respected Sheppard, I'll go along with you."

"Leo," Eugene stammered, "I'm doing it to preserve our race!"

"Yes, you are, but that goes far beyond killing one man. We condone violence only for the purpose of self-protection, not as a personal vendetta." Leo then took the stage. "Men, we all know that this worldwide organization has to turn the other cheek sometimes and, gentlemen, that's what I'm asking you to do right now. Forget about this meeting!"

Eugene stood there stunned. The effects of the liquor completely gone now, he couldn't believe that Leo had contradicted him in front of everyone. And now the group may have lost respect for him and what he had tried to get across to his fellow Sheppards.

"Leo, how could you do that?" Eugene said, stung by Leo's actions.

"Eugene, we have a respectable membership here. Now they may not love mud people, but they have too much to lose by going after one powerless nigger. If you want to kill a snake, Eugene, you have to chop off its head—not its tail."

"I see. So is that how you feel, my friend?"

"Like I said, Eugene, I'll work with you, but not my group. You can use Mel Rose and his people."

"That'll be fine. Now excuse me!" Eugene was frustrated, but well aware of the powder keg he was sitting on, so he quietly went over to the coffeepot and poured himself a cup. Things certainly were not going as planned.

Mom had reached Dad before I told him to move. I had frightened Dad so much that he and the girls fled with only the clothes they were wearing and whatever they could load into the small U-Haul trailer Dad had rented. Dad was pleased that I had left him the Sunbird. It gave him mobility. Dad wouldn't buy his own car because he felt that he could live without it, but having the Sunbird was a blessing. Dad arranged to have all the utilities shut off. Leaving so much behind was painful, but he realized that whoever had shot me would go after him as well. And he had to protect his girls.

Charlotte had learned from Theo that I had been shot. She insisted that Theo and the girls come to Utah. At first, Theo balked. He didn't want to take the girls out of school in the middle of the year, but he talked with the high school principal, and the principal said that if Theo made it to Utah within the week, special consideration would be given to the girls so they wouldn't fall behind in their studies. Theo thanked the principal and got the girls ready to leave.

Pal took it hard. He asked to go with them. Theo felt the young man's pain, but he couldn't bring Pal with them and he couldn't risk leaving his daughter here for these fools to harm or even kill. So he promised Pal that he'd keep an eye on Daisy. Pal reluctantly agreed and he and Daily said their tearful farewells. With the Sunbird hitched, Theo and the girls left Seattle at 10:30 Friday morning.

With Leo's permission, Eugene had organized six soldiers to do his dirty work. Eugene realized that he would have to use his own money. He offered each man $10,000 for his services. Mel Rose was in charge, and Eugene promised him $20,000. "My fellow Sheppards, I want you to infiltrate two addresses. I want you to either maim or put the residents six feet under, gentlemen. And no witnesses!"

This was his final stand. Anne and Casey would have to die, too. He had lost his wife and daughter, but he was going to impose his will on them to prove that he was the superior; his way was the best.

At 10:00 p.m. that Saturday night, Mel led the men over to Roger's house in central Seattle. The porchlights were off. Mel took out his nine millimeter and addressed the two men who were with him, Tory Whitaker and Marvin Beal. "Okay, I want you to go around the back and get into the house. Once you're inside, if you see someone, use one of these hunting knives."

"We'll cut them in two with these babies!"

"Be careful, Whitaker. He's armed!" Mel didn't want to take any chances. The two men stealthily crept out of the white van. Eugene had let Mel keep it for now. In this neighborhood no one asked questions or stuck their nose into anyone else's business. When Tory and Marvin kicked the back door open, they found that the home was pitch black. Tory went back to the van and asked Mel for a flashlight. Now he could see. They searched the home, but found no one. Finally, Marvin said, "I think it's empty, Tory."

"I think you're right."

Both men laughed, and then began to slash and destroy everything they could. They spent twenty minutes ransacking the place and then went back to the van. Mel contemplated the situation and then said harshly, "Torch the place!"

"Okay, boss." The men took a two-gallon gas container and went back inside. They poured the gasoline over everything that looked flammable and then lit it. They ran out as the fire slowly gained strength. When they reached the van, Mel could see the fire through the blinds.

Whitaker and Beal were young, eager teenagers, trying to prove themselves to the older guys. Tory Whitaker was a sixteen-year-old, slight of build and still in the goofy stages of growing up, when getting high and laughing were of the utmost importance. His premature cigarette smoking overshadowed his boyish charm. The kid had a lot to learn to make it as a Sheppard. To him it was all a game. Marvin Beal, on the other hand, had solid potential. A well-built youth, Marvin was a serious boy. He could have been a businessman, but his all-consuming hatred of inferior races had stunted his development. He liked girls, and with his curly blond hair and piercing blue eyes, he had nailed a few of them. As Mel drove away, he handed the youths an open bottle of gin.

Kent Gardener agreed to check Casey's apartment. In this neighborhood, you had to be careful, though. People watched each other's backs here. The best he could do was to put a few rounds into the windows. He would drive by the apartment and let Kyle and Tim do the shooting. Both of them had been with Mel and Kent when they'd accosted Roger and the Chinaman. Kent remembered the situation well. He chuckled at the memory.

"Okay, fellas, I'm going to stop and you two run out. Get as close to the apartment as you can, and fire as many rounds into the place as possible." When Kent neared Casey's, he slowed down the stolen '87 Cordova. Both Kyle and Tim jumped out. With the silencers in place, they crept right up to the windows and emptied the clips of the nine millimeters. After the weapons were empty, the two men ran for the Cordova. Kent eased away from the scene.

When Eugene got word of the hits, he was still upset. He wasn't sure what to do next. He had no bodies to prove that the hits had been successful. Now he'd have to wait. He decided to rent a hotel room—damn living with Leo. Eugene had soured on the man.

Casey's neighbor, Carolyn White, was a single woman in her thirties. She'd always respected Casey, even though Casey was living with a black man. Carolyn felt that trouble might come, so every now and then, she watched for things. She knew Casey was out of town, so she was surprised to see men approaching Casey's door. In horror, Carolyn watched from her window as the two men pulled out weapons and began firing into Casey's apartment. Carolyn fell to the floor, crawled over to the phone, and called the police.

This apartment was familiar to Hank Albright: Roger Singleton and Casey Balkner lived here. As he approached the apartment, he looked over the place. The windows had been shattered by dozens of bullets. Hank was curious about how extensive the damage was inside. He knocked on Carolyn's door first. She opened it, and said, "Are you with the police?"

"Yes, ma'am. Did you call?"

"Yes, I did."

"My name's Detective Albright, ma'am." Hank showed Carolyn his badge.

"Yes, come in, detective. I called because I saw two men approach my next-door neighbor's apartment and began shooting into it. It scared me so I called."

"You did the right thing, ma'am. Did you get a look at the perpetrators?

"Yes, they were both relatively young, white kids, and the weapons didn't make much noise. The shots sounded muffled, like a hammer hitting a nail."

"I see. Well, can you describe the men, ma'am?"

"I can try." Carolyn thought about what she'd seen. "From what I saw in the streetlight, both men were of average height, around 5 foot 9 or so. They had on military-type outfits and both appeared to be rather young. And oh, yes, detective, they came from a car, but I can't say what type of car except that it was a dark color, maybe blue or black."

Hank Albright couldn't put the puzzle together just yet. The two white youths did not appear to have any connection to the Gillione murders. He took the report from Miss White and told her to be careful.

Miss White then said, "You know, detective, I don't mean to sound gossipy, but the black man who lives there. . . he does keep odd hours. I thought you should know."

Hank Albright thought about Roger's shooting and asked, "Did you see or hear anything, say, close to a month ago?"

"I was spending some time over in Oregon then."

"Well, call us if you hear or see anything else, alright?"

"Oh, I'll be sure to do that, detective."

"Okay, now, you stay inside the rest of the night. Hopefully, they won't come back."

"Good-bye, detective."

"Night, ma'am," Albright said.

The detective went over to Casey's apartment and peered through the broken windows. Besides the broken glass and bullet holes in the furniture and walls, nothing appeared to have been touched. Albright was fairly certainly that the gunmen hadn't gone inside.

As Albright left the apartment complex, he began to see the outlines of an ugly web being woven. First Gillione had been murdered, and now Roger Singleton seemed to be a target. Albright concentrated hard as he was driving away from the crime scene. He'd let the foot soldiers search for clues in the apartment that was shot up. For now, he'd go and question Madeline Thompson.

The crime scene investigators arrived after Albright had left the area. They knocked on Casey's door repeatedly and got no answer. Carolyn came outside and told them that no one was home. The CSI techs marked the front door with yellow tape. When the occupants of the apartment came back, they'd know to summon the police.

Albright called Madeline Thompson and asked to speak to her. Madeline agreed. What did she have to lose? It was well after midnight, and Madeline was getting sleepy. She wondered if the detective would ever get there. Finally, at about 1:30 in the morning, Albright arrived. Madeline was looking out her window and quickly opened the door for him. "Come in, detective."

"Thanks, ma'am. I had a few questions to ask you."

"Okay."

"What can you tell me about Roger Singleton?"

"I worked with Roger at the Haven for a while. We were friends, if you could call it that."

"Miss Thompson, what were Roger's habits?"

"He would always go downtown during his lunch break and stay the whole hour."

"Do you know what he did?"

"Well, detective. I'm not sure, but he could have been selling drugs."

"What makes you think so?" The light was beginning to dawn.

"He always talked to a Chinese guy who stopped by here from time to time." That statement jolted Albright. He knew the Chinese Dragons were a dangerous gang who could be formidable adversaries, even for the Seattle police. "Miss Thompson, I need a name."

"Well, detective, I heard Roger on the phone once and he mentioned the name 'Chu.'"

"Thank you. Miss Thompson. I'll be in touch. Get some sleep."

"You're welcome, detective."

As Albright left Madeline's apartment, he felt as if he were sitting on a powder keg. If he could get hold of Chu, he'd be in business. Albright decided to wait until morning. Then he'd speak to Chu.

Ten-thirty Sunday morning. Albright was up and about. He had driven over to the Chinese section of Seattle. Albright knew of Won Chu, a dangerous man who had ties to the syndicate. Men disappeared when they asked Chu or any other player the wrong questions. Albright figured he'd stick to the story about Roger for now. As Albright approached the place he was looking for, he slowed down. He spotted Chu walking by himself near some apartment buildings, and couldn't believe his good fortune.

The detective got out of the car and yelled to the Chinese man, "Hey, excuse me." The man turned around, and to Albright's surprise it wasn't Chu at all; it was a Chinaman, but he was too young to fit Chu's description. However, Albright could probably get a warrant; this Chinese gang leader was as hot as hot coal.

"Excuse me, son. I'm Detective Hank Albright, Seattle Police. Can you tell me where I can find Won Chu?"

The young Chinese man studied Albright, and said, "I can't tell you anything, man!" Hank had to think fast. He said, "Look, I think you should come to the station. We need to talk."

"For what officer? What did I do?"

"Turn around!" Albright ordered.

The young man turned around docilely, and Albright handcuffed him without incident. He slowly drove the young man to the station. It was a terrible thing to do, but the detective needed answers. When they arrived at the station, Albright opened the door. His ploy was working—the Chinese man now looked frightened. Albright played his hand. "I just want some answers. Do you know Won Chu?" No answer. "Make it easy on yourself. Do you know him?" Albright sized up the diminutive young man, who wore jeans and a T-shirt.

"Alright, officer, alright!" The young man seemed ready to comply.

"What do you want from Chu, man?"

"All I want is to ask him some questions about Roger Singleton."

"Okay, I'll call him, and you ask him from there." Albright took out his cell phone and gave it to the young man. "By the way, what's your name?"

"The name is Su Lee, officer." Su Lee dialed the number and waited for a reply. Finally, it was answered. "Yeah!" Su Lee became nervous.

"Hello, Chu, this is Su Lee."

"What can I do for you, Lee?"

"Well, I have a detective here who wants to ask you about Roger."

"What about Roger?" Chu began to get irritated.

"I don't know, Chu, but he wants to talk to you."

"Put him on the phone!" Chu said sternly. Lee handed Albright the cell phone.

"Detective Albright speaking. Look, Chu, someone is trying to kill Roger. Can you help me?"

Chu began to get nervous. "Why are you asking me about it, detective?"

"I thought maybe you could help me, Chu. I need answers!"

"Well, officer, Roger works for me. We are janitors."

"Do you know why anyone would want to kill him?" Chu thought for a second, and then said, "Yeah, he had some trouble with some people calling themselves Sheppards or something."

"Thanks, Chu."

"Put Lee back on the line, officer."

Albright reluctantly handed the phone back to Lee.

Chu firmly reprimanded the young man. "Lee, next time, you'd better leave me out of this or else!" Chu hung up.

Lee looked very frightened as he gave Albright the phone. "Thanks a lot, officer, for everything." Lee said menacingly.

"You're welcome," Albright said, smiling.

Lee quickly left thinking what could he have done? The cop had him in a corner. Now Lee would have to answer to the most feared man in his world.

When Albright got word that Roger Singleton's home had been torched, he knew what was going on. Several Seattle policemen were Sheppards, but Albright didn't know much about the group, except that it was a white supremacist organization. Mentioning the Sheppards to fellow officers might open up a nasty can of vipers. Only one man could help him, and that was the state senator. Albright was pretty much on his own, so he'd better keep this to himself.

Alfredo

CHAPTER 13

THE THUG

Gillione's people took the loss hard. Gillione had been an important part of the Parillo family. They had come to America from Italy over thirty years ago. Raymond Gillione was a key player on the West Coast. Without him the Parillo family would have to send someone else out to Seattle. Alfredo Martin, a local thug, did odd jobs for the Parillo family. Jobs like breaking bones and knocking out teeth. He wasn't above killing, which was something he'd done on several occasions.

Alfredo had received a message from Don Parillo a couple of days ago, instructing him to meet Don at the pool hall on 67th Street that Wednesday. The pool hall catered mainly to spics and niggers, but they didn't bother you if they knew you, and Alfredo knew just about everyone in this part of New Jersey. Alfredo knew that Ollie's Pool Queue was the perfect place to discuss business.

When Alfredo arrived at the pool hall, it was not at the peak hour. Things really started rolling at around nine o'clock, so Alfredo and Parillo had a couple of hours almost to themselves. Alfredo was in the rear of the huge building, drinking a beer.

Don Parillo, all 6 foot 6 of him, stood in the doorway. Don looked the place over before going inside. He made a motion with his head, and two well-built men wearing dark shades walked in. That was Parillo's muscle. As Alfredo watched the scene unfold, he was slightly amused. This was Parillo's way of showing that he was not one to be trifled with. Parillo finally spotted Alfredo and headed toward him.

"Alfie, how are you?"

Alfredo stood up and embraced his boss. "Fine, Donny, just fine. How's the family?"

"The family is beautiful, Alfie."

Don Parillo sat down across from Alfredo. Alfredo took his seat, and watched as the two bodyguards started a game of pool on one of the many empty pool tables.

"Look, Alfie, I'm sorry to drag you into my personal affairs, but I need some answers. My good friend Raymond Gillione was whacked, and I can't let this go without getting to the bottom of it."

"What do you want me to do, Donny?"

"I want you to live long, have many children, see lots of things, but, my friend, I need you to take care of something for me."

"Anything, Donny." Alfredo made a living using his muscle. He was short on money just now, and desperately needed some. Doing a job for Don Parillo could mean thousands.

"Alfie, I need you to go to Seattle for me and look into the death of my friend, Raymond Gillione. I just want to know who did it. If you have to, flex some muscle, but don't ice anyone. Not yet, anyway." Alfredo nodded. Parillo went on, "You see Alfie, Raymond Gillione had some two hundred pounds of smack when they hit him, and now it's missing. I want to know who has it."

"Alright, Donny. I'll go to the West Coast and look into it. You got any names?"

"Yes. A Chinaman by the name of Won Chu, and I hear he's very busy in Seattle's red-light district."

"There's a guy who owes me in LA. I'll get the lowdown on Chu from him before I head up to Seattle. OK?"

"Sound like a plan.

And Alfie?"

"Yes?"

"See what Chu knows about Raymond Gillione."

Don slipped an inch-thick envelope into Alfredo's hand. "A little something for the trip." Don Parillo's bodyguards stopped shooting pool as soon as they saw their boss stand up. The three of them quickly left the establishment.

Alfredo looked around the pool hall. There were about fifteen or twenty guys in the place, and they all seemed to be hard cases. Alfredo sipped his beer as he felt his pulse rise. He stood 6 foot 3 and weighed a solid 240 pounds. Some fat, but mainly muscle. Alfredo had spent eight years in the penitentiary for manslaughter—it was the only murder that he'd ever been caught for. He'd killed a man for giving him the wrong directions while he was in the Bronx selling some paintings he'd stolen from a pawnshop. After Alfredo went down the wrong street, three thieves grabbed both paintings. The paintings were worth thousands, and after a vicious struggle, Alfredo was cut across the right cheek with a dull razor. When he found the man who'd given him the wrong directions, Alfredo choked him to death. As the man fought for his last breath, he managed to say, "I just moved here, man!" It was too late; Alfredo had finished him off. He had crushed the man's windpipe.

The police found Alfredo drunk and incoherent, and he confessed to the killing the next day. Turned out, the man was a drifter from Boston. Alfredo never mentioned the paintings. But the four-inch scar that ran down his cheek required twenty stitches. The judge decided that eight years was a gift.

Alfredo served every minute of his time. While inside, he made lots of friends. He had gotten in contact with the Parillo family through Luther Perez, a Puerto Rican native, who was a runner for them. Luther thought Alfredo looked tough enough, and that he wasn't the snitch type, so he gave Alfredo a number to call if he needed work when he got out of the joint. Upon his release six years ago, Alfredo had called the number. Don Parillo trusted Luther's judgment, and Alfredo had been working for Parillo ever since.

Alfredo continued to check out the patrons of the pool hall and noticed that one group of them had branched off and were whispering among themselves. He remembered his first job for Don Parillo. Parillo, a tall and slim man, was a legitimate businessman; he had a limousine service. Parillo had over one hundred prime vehicles that mostly served the well-to-do. Parillo had been married three times, but according to legend, he remained faithful to each wife during the marriage. Parillo, at fifty, looked much younger than his years. His close-cropped, jet-black hair went well with his olive complexion. He could pass for Mexican, but Parillo was from the old country. He had told Alfredo many tales of Sicily over dinner. Alfredo was impressed. Parillo took an instant liking to the mixed-breed Alfredo Martin. Born of a black mother and a Caucasian father, Alfredo had seen his share of hard times. He loved his mother dearly. Alfredo had three younger sisters. Even though he was considered a criminal, his sisters adored their big brother. His reputation as a bone breaker kept would-be suitors at a respectful distance from his family.

One of Parillo's bodyguards, Vincent Macione, knew about Alfredo's toughness firsthand. The two had had a previous run-in. At one of Parillo's parties, Vincent had tried to intimidate Alfredo. When the skirmish was over, Vincent, a bloodied mess, threw his hands up in surrender. To Alfredo, Vincent didn't deserve a position of trust in the organization. A runt with a round stomach, and exceptionally homely, Vincent couldn't fight worth a damn. His only advantage was that he carried a piece wherever he went. Vincent was a distant relative of Parillo's, so he was an insider. Alfredo didn't recognize the other bodyguard. However, he looked like a guy who could handle himself anywhere.

One of the men in the group off to the side approached Alfredo. "Hey, man, what you plan on doing about leaving this joint with all that money?"

Alfredo eyed the black man closely. Alfredo needed some people to go to Seattle with him. So he said, "Hey, I need some guys to help me with a job, comprende?"

"What's the deal, partner? Is it serious or something light?"

Alfredo sized up the black man, who had a slight build and who looked like drugs or hard living had taken its toll. He was smiling at Alfredo.

Alfredo spoke slowly and quietly. "Look, you round up, say, three of your hardest boys, and I'll guarantee a thousand bucks apiece. It's a two-week job."

"A thousand bucks apiece? Yeah, man, I'll do that. Give me a number that I can reach you at." Alfredo wrote down his number on a napkin. "Call me at 8:00 tomorrow morning."

"By the way, stranger, I need an advance."

Alfredo looked into the envelope; it was filled with $100 bills. Alfredo gave the lean, haggard-looking black man $200.

"Damn, partner, you keep it coming like this, and we'll be in business for a long time!"

"Just call me, _____?" Alfredo gestured for a name.

"Mack, Mack Warren."

"Okay, Mack, be talking to you tomorrow." As Mack walked away, Alfredo watched him go to the bar and order drinks for his boys. This was Alfredo's cue to leave.

When Alfredo got home, he called Watts in California. He wanted to talk with T-Bone Collins. Collins was a distributor throughout California and parts of Oregon and Washington. Alfredo got hold of Sam, one of T-Bone's flunkies. "Hello?"

"Hello, who is this?"

"This is Alfredo Martin from Jersey."

"What you want?"

"I need to speak to T-Bone." Alfredo knew how difficult it was to talk to T-Bone because of T-Bone's paranoia.

"T-Bone isn't taking calls right now."

"Look, I have some serious information for Bone, now let me get with him, yo?"

"What you say your name is?"

"T-Bone knows me as Alfie."

Seconds later, he came on the line. "Hello, this is Bone, and this better be good!"

"Hey, Bone, this is Alfie!"

"Alfie, long time, no see. How're things?"

"You know, shitty as usual."

"Yeah, I know the drill."

"Look, Bone, I'm coming out to Cali in a couple of days or so. Can we get together?"

"Alfie, I know we go back a ways, but I'm a busy man. Anyway, why're you coming all the way out here?"

"I'm trying to find out about someone."

"Is it business or pleasure, Alfie?"

"I'd like it to be pleasure, but that's not it. I'm on a job."

"Knowing you, Alfie, someone is going to be sorry as hell that you came."

"Look, Bone, I just need a few names and locations, and I'll be out of your hair."

"What's in it for me?"

"We can call it even, Bone."

"Oh, yeah, I do owe you one." After a short pause, Bone said, "Meet me in three days in front of the abandoned apartments on 110th Street. Bring a cell phone, man, so I can call you if you get lost."

"Sounds good, Bone. See you then!" Both men hung up. Alfredo wrote down the address. He had met T-Bone while they were both men were incarcerated in a New York state prison. T-Bone was a likable guy; he was serving five years for drug distribution. He told Alfredo that when he got out of prison, he was going to make it big in California. Alfredo didn't think much of Bone's plan, but he gave T-Bone his blessings.

In the penitentiary, the two men took a liking to each other. On one occasion T-Bone had walked into the wrong section. He had wandered into the homosexual wing while he was horsing around. They had tied T-Bone down and ripped his clothes off. They had him naked and were ready to go at him. Alfredo, who was housed near the scene, happened to be informed by his cronies that his boy T-Bone was about to be raped. Alfredo rushed to the scene with three buddies, and the homosexuals fled, leaving T-Bone tied up, naked and screaming. T-Bone made a vow to Alfredo that if there was anything he could do to repay Alfredo, he would do it. Now Alfredo was cashing in.

Alfredo started packing an overnight bag. He wasn't trying to impress anybody; he was just going to find out what Won Chu had to do with Gillione's execution.

Alfredo woke up at five o'clock the next morning. He fixed himself a light breakfast and then went out and checked his car. It was a good-running, green, '98 Oldsmobile Cutlass Supreme, which Alfredo had learned to trust. He checked the car over and went back inside to wait for Mack's call. The job across country would be a change for Alfredo—something he longed for.

Alfredo began thinking of his days of working for Don Parillo. Alfredo had earned his stripes. His first job was one he would never forget. He had been sent to pick up $25,000 from a drug dealer. When Alfredo made contact with the trembling teenager, who seemed barely in his teens, Alfredo muscled the boy out of $3,000. Don had told Alfredo to rough Skipper up a little bit, but Alfredo realized that Skipper, a sickly boy, might not survive a beating. His health appeared to be very precarious. Skipper was young, white, boyish-looking, and uneducated; he ran a respectable powdered-cocaine distribution ring. Alfredo had to respect the kid's ingenuity. Skipper had several felons on a tight leash that were selling for him, and he had excellent connections with Don Parillo. Skipper made all the arrangements, while the felons under his command ran the drugs. Alfredo had forced Skipper to tell him everything. Alfredo had caught Skipper alone and really needled him.

The phone rang. It was Mack Warren. "Hey, this Alfredo?"

"Yeah, speak!"

"I'm calling about the job, man!"

Alfredo tensed and then said, "Are we still on?"

"Hey, Alfredo, me and my man Snook, we'll take you up on the job. Don't worry: Two of us will be plenty for you, man!"

"Have you ever worked for anybody, Mack?"

"I'm the one they call the Avenger in these parts. I can handle anything that comes my way!"

"Well, Mack, meet me at the pool hall in thirty minutes and we'll talk again."

"I'll be there. Later."

Alfredo had heard of the Avenger, a blood-thirsty coke fiend who would kill his own brother for a hit, but he was thorough. He'd finish the job. Alfredo looked around the apartment. It was a two-room affair in the slums of Trenton, New Jersey. Alfredo had learned to love the ghetto style of life. You could be as lawless as you wanted and still be a respected citizen. Alfredo rarely worried about the law. New Jersey police, while efficient, let this part of the city police itself. The city was viewed as a food chain, and the meanest beast ruled. Alfredo liked that theory, since he considered himself one mean beast.

His mother and sisters were over in the Bronx, staying with his uncle for a week. Joseph Addison was a relatively respectable man; he drove trucks for a living. Alfredo's mother, Sarah Addison, took care of her brother's place while he was on the road.

The girls—Nadine, Beatrice, and Connie—were still children; all were under eighteen. Connie was the youngest at thirteen. But their age didn't matter because the guys in Trenton still chased them. Alfredo knew that he could protect them for only so long, and then the girls would be on their own. Alfredo wanted them to settle down in a legitimate life. The girls were street smart. They had little use for school, something that troubled Alfredo. He feared that the cold streets would come back and bite them.

Sarah tried to help Joseph as much as possible. Although he drank quite heavily, Joseph was a decent man. He had driven trucks for twenty-eight years. He never had an accident, and he understood money. Joseph played the money-market accounts well, and he received $15,000 a month—work or no work. Sarah knew this and did everything in her power to stay on Joseph's good side. Joseph practically raised the girls. He considered them his own. Joseph thought Alfredo was a thug, but he understood that, for some, if you didn't prey on others, you yourself would become a victim.

Taking one last look at his apartment, Alfredo went to meet Mack. Mack and Snook were waiting at the pool hall. Alfredo pulled into the parking lot. The horrors of ghetto life only fueled the ambition of men like these. They no longer searched for equal rights, but sought to get ahead by any means at hand. Alfredo motioned for the two men to get into the car.

Mack spoke first. "So what's the gig, man?"

Alfredo carefully sized him up, then said, "I need to go to the West Coast for a few days, and I need some eyes and ears."

Mack replied confidently, "Look, man, for a thousand dollars, I'd be your girl!"

"This the first time you been on a job, Mack?"

"Man, I have been on the streets for thirty-two years. I've hustled, I've robbed, I've been legit, but mainly I work for whoever pays the right price."

That sounded good to Alfredo, who said, "We'll go to the West Coast for a week. You do what I say, and work with me, and I'll make it worth your while." Snook sat in the back seat, smelly and quiet, observing this exchange.

Now that he had his employees for the job, Alfredo sat silent, waiting for a reply.

Mack gave it to him. "We're game, man. Just say the word and we're there!"

Alfredo smiled, turned on the ignition, and headed for Don Parillo's garage.

Casey

CHAPTER 14

THE BREAKUP

Casey couldn't believe her eyes. The apartment had been shot up. They had just made it to Seattle. She looked around the living room. Bullet holes were in the walls. Paintings of substantial value had been damaged. Her leather couch had several holes in it. The television had exploded after being hit by one of the bullets. As Casey straightened things up she couldn't help but cry.

Anne tried to console her daughter. "It's okay, Casey. We'll get through this."

"No, it's not okay, Mom!"

I sat there in disbelief. I wanted to confront Eugene and ask, "Why?" But I knew that would be pointless. "Casey, we both know why your dad is doing this."

"Yes, Roger, but to fire guns in my place means he wanted me dead, too."

Anne then added, "You know, Casey, he wanted all of us dead."

"I don't feel like talking right now, Mom." Casey saw how self-centered she had become. Even though she loved me, she began to loathe me and our relationship.

"Casey," Anne said, "you're under a lot of pressure. Maybe you should take a nap."

"No, Mom, I'm calling the police!" Casey dialed Hank Albright's number.

"Detective Albright, Seattle Police."

"Yes, this is Casey Balkner."

"Hello, Miss Balkner, how are you?"

"I'm fine, detective, thanks," Casey said, her voice trembling with fear and anger.

"Look, Miss Balkner, I know you've had trouble with things. It looks like Mr. Singleton is a target. I suggest that you find another place to live for now. And, Miss Balkner, someone burned Mr. Singleton's home."

"Oh, no," Casey moaned. "Was there anybody inside?"

"No, but the place was trashed before it was set on fire."

"Do you have any leads, detective?"

"I'm not at liberty to say, ma'am."

"I see. So in the meantime, I should go into hiding?"

"Yes, Miss Balkner that would be wise." Albright didn't want to sound corny, but this was all he had to work with.

"Well, I'll be in touch. Thank you, Detective Albright." Casey looked over at me, sitting on the only chair that hadn't been damaged.

"Roger, someone burned down your house."

"Are you serious? Damn!" I thought about my father. "Was anyone inside?"

"No."

"Good!" I quickly called my mother in Utah, and learned that my father and sisters were there. That was a relief. Then I called Chu.

Chu was relieved to hear from me. "I thought you were dead, my friend!"

"No, I'm still here, Chu."

"By the way, Roger, the police asked me about you. Why me?"

"Chu, I'm just getting back from Philly and Cleveland—I really don't know. And that last night you dropped me off, I was shot. That's why I haven't been in touch."

"What's going on?"

"I don't know, Chu. I really don't know!"

"Well, keep in touch, Roger. And be careful, my friend."

"I will. Later, Chu." I contemplated my next move. With my homeowner's insurance I'd probably get an insurance settlement sometime soon. Then I had a flash. "Casey, I'm going to Utah. Forget this madness!"

Casey was thinking about her life. With the way things were going, she felt that she and I had different goals. We'd never be able to live in peace. "Look Roger," Casey said, "I can give you some money, if you want. I think I'll go back to Cleveland."

"Why? To be with Allen Wilson?" I saw it all slipping away. "Your father has gotten to you, Casey."

"Yeah."

Anne could see the strain between Casey and me, so she kept quiet. Let them settle their dispute, just the two of them.

"Roger, I'm sorry, but this is too much. I can't take it anymore."

"I know, Casey." I went over and held my lady; she was shaking with fear and anger. Splitting up right now would be for the best. "Casey, I could use a few thousand just to get by. I'll pay you back." My stash of $15,000 was in my Sunbird—thank goodness for that.

"Okay, Roger, but I'll have to go to the bank to get it." Casey seemed to calm down, and after she composed herself, she and Anne went to the local Washington Mutual branch.

My leg was getting stronger. Leaving Casey at this point was the right course for both of us. I began to pack my belongings for the trip to Utah. I would take my thirty-eight with me. I decided to call Chu, my only real friend. Selling crack left me with no one I could count on. Besides Casey and my family, I was all alone in this world. "Chu, I need to ask you a big favor."

"What is it, Roger?"

"I need you to take me to Utah, Chu. Tonight!"

"Hey, Roger, who do you know in Utah?"

"My family."

"Things getting a little hot, huh?"

"I'm tired, Chu."

"I understand, Roger. Look, I'll be by in a couple of hours."

"That's fine. I'll be waiting." It was early May. Casey and I were bending under Eugene's relentless pressure. I could take only so much harassment before it broke my spirit. Maybe Casey felt that way, too.

Casey and Anne tried to work things out. They both realized that, unwittingly, I had broken up their family. Eugene wouldn't forgive, but she missed being a family. The two women didn't talk much on the drive to the bank; they were busy sorting things out. When they got to the bank, one of Eugene's people saw them. He immediately phoned Eugene. Eugene's spirits perked up, and he called Mel Rose. "Mel, they're back. Now I want you to earn your money!"

"What do you want me to do?"

"Catch them and kill them!"

"Where, Eugene?"

"At their apartment, dammit. I don't care where—just do it!"

"I'll get them when they get back to the apartment." Mel hung up and got going. He grabbed his trusty nine millimeter and some spare clips and headed out. He would do this by himself. It was 3:30 in the afternoon, and Mel knew that there would be people milling around. I'll shoot and then get the hell away from the scene, Mel thought.

Hank Albright had parked his car behind the apartment complex. The Sheppards were trying to kill Roger Singleton-why, he didn't know—but it was his job to protect and serve. Albright was waiting behind the apartment shrubbery. His instincts told him that trouble was brewing. Casey withdrew $6,000 from her account. She'd give me half and keep half for herself. She and Anne would look up Allen Wilson in Cleveland.

When they got back to the apartment, Casey and Anne stepped out of the car. As they neared Casey's apartment, a white van came out of nowhere, the driver pulled up next to Anne and Casey, and he took aim. Albright spotted the van and stepped out into the open. Casey and Anne instinctively dropped to the ground. Albright fired eight slugs into the van. The van veered out of control and rammed into a parked car. Mel had been hit several times in the chest, and died instantly. Albright raced to the van, and with his weapon drawn he approached the driver's side door. When the driver didn't respond to Albright's command to drop his weapon, the detective went in closer, and checked Mel's pulse, confirming that Mel was dead. Then he made sure Anne and Casey weren't hurt, and he went back to his car to radio in.

Three squad cars were there within fifteen minutes. Meanwhile, I had come outside. Casey and Anne were visibly shaken, so I went over to them.

"Roger, we just . . ." Casey had lost the ability to speak. I held her and Anne. Albright came over to the three of us.

"I'm very sorry, people, but something terrible is going on here. Can any of you help me figure out what it is?" No one spoke, so Albright added, "I know about the Sheppards. Does that ring a bell?"

"Look, detective, this is something I really don't know how to explain," Casey said. Albright pointed to the coroners removing the Mel Rose's body. "That guy. Do you know him?"

I walked over to take a look. After gasping, I blurted out, "That's the one of the guys who jumped me several months back."

Albright sized up the situation. Mel Rose must have been working for the Sheppards. The grim reality of this case was settling in on the detective. The world was closing in on him. Once the policemen who belonged to the Sheppards found out about this, Albright might just be in big trouble. He suggested that Casey, Anne, and I find someplace else to stay for the night. We all agreed.

I had called the insurance company and put in a claim on my burned home. I was told that I'd have to file a written claim, and then afterwards, an official investigation would take place. This would take up to six weeks and then I'd be notified about a settlement. I could make it until then. Casey gave me the $3,000, which I accepted and put away. All I had to do now was wait for Chu. When Chu arrived at 7:30 p.m., I was ready. I took Casey in my arms and said, "I love you, Casey. I always will."

"I love you too, Roger." Casey began to cry.

Anne added, "You'll always be in my heart, Roger." Anne came over and hugged me. I felt the tears falling. I picked up my suitcases and said good-bye. I kissed both women and headed for Chu's van.

When Eugene heard that Mel Rose had been killed, he felt nauseated. This wasn't part of the plan. Eugene could either continue to throw people at me, or he could lay low. The informant was Officer Lynn Summers. Eugene wanted to know where I was going, but for now he'd get some much-needed rest.

Casey and Anne packed as quickly as they could. They threw their luggage in the trunk and began the long journey back to Cleveland; hopefully, Allen Wilson would be waiting.

Casey's heart was with me, but she had been through so much with me that it had soured our relationship. Casey had talked to her mom about marriage, but that wasn't going to happen now. They might be seeing me for the last time. Casey's belongings were important, but she had to cut her losses somewhere; she still had both her mother's and her own life to think about. Getting away from Eugene was paramount.

The chief questioned Hank Albright. It was apparent that Mel Rose was a hired hit man, but who was he working for? Albright said, "The Sheppards, sir."

"Are you sure, Albright?"

"I'm positive, chief." Chief José Rodriguez was a fair man. He had been police chief for over five years. Now, Detective Hank Albright was telling him that the Sheppards were responsible for this hit man. "Why did the Sheppards hire him, detective?"

"So they could kill a black man, sir."

"I see. Again, detective, why would they want this particular black man dead?"

"He's done something to them, sir."

"Okay. Detective, when you shot the suspect, who was he aiming at?"

"Two females, sir. Both white."

"This doesn't make sense. I still can't see how the Sheppards could be involved." If it was the one thing José had learned, it was not to mess with secret organizations—especially white ones. A person didn't last long if he did. Not only was José street-smart, but he had risen through the ranks by hard work and by following procedure. He wasn't prepared for this. "Look, detective, I'm going to place you on administrative leave until there's a review. Got it?"

"Got it, chief." Reluctantly, Hank Albright accepted his situation. He'd just been doing his job, and now he was in hot water.

"I wouldn't say anything about this theory of yours that the Sheppards were responsible for this, if I were you. That's for your own good."

"Certainly, chief." Hank Albright walked out of the chief's office a little frazzled. He noticed the stares he was getting from the other officers as he walked through the precinct. Life would never be the same, Albright thought.

Eugene had a fifth of Scotch to drown his sorrow. He was responsible for a man's death, and the nigger was still alive. Anne and Casey had escaped. All he could do now was cut his losses and pick up the pieces or he could continue to hunt down Roger, Allen Wilson, and his family. Lynn Summers had told him that, even though the Sheppards were linked to the drive-by, pinning something on them now would be difficult. No one would come forward to testify against them. Eugene took another drink. He put the bottle down and fell back on the bed. He'd have to settle for dreaming about achieving his goals.

Eugene woke up with a nasty hangover. The motel room he had rented was a real doozy. Leo knew where he was, but what Eugene didn't know was that Leo had contacted headquarters over in Europe. Leo had explained to the Grand Sheppards that Eugene was out of control, and that he needed to be reprimanded or eliminated. Eugene had lost his sanity and the only way to bring him back to his senses was by forcing the issue.

As Eugene showered and got dressed, he turned on the television set. He watched a little bit of the news and after only several seconds, he angrily shut the television off. He called room service and ordered some coffee. As he waited for the coffee, he was surprised to hear someone knocking on the door so quickly. As he opened it, three masked men rushed into the room and put a pillowcase over Eugene's head. Eugene instantly knew that this was the "kiss of death." Still, he pleaded for his life. "Please," Eugene whined, "I only wanted to preserve our heritage!" Eugene understood that to warrant the kiss of death, a member of the Sheppards would have to be viewed as a danger to the integrity of the Sheppards; still, Eugene didn't want to die. As Eugene's hands were tied behind his back, Eugene heard a revolver cylinder spinning. He heard the hammer click back then he braced for the explosion.

Click, click. Terrified, Eugene realized that they were playing Russian roulette with him. Then Eugene heard a voice, a smooth alto, a deeply educated voice.

"Brother Balkner, Brother Balkner, you have seriously used the fellowship contrary to your sworn pledge. You know what that means, don't you, Eugene?"

"Look, fellas, I thought that the purpose of the fellowship was to keep Aryan blood pure."

"You forgot one thing. You took a vow never to jeopardize the organization's anonymity. Sorry, Eugene."

Click, click. Eugene wet his pants. Seconds later, he heard footsteps leading away from him.

The next thing he heard was a female voice politely saying, "Here's your coffee, sir." The cute young clerk, Mandy Patterson, had been working at the hotel for three months. She had never seen the three men outside of Mr. Balkner's room before. Alarmed at first, Mandy wanted to inform the manager, but when they offered her $50 to act as though they weren't there, Mandy was relieved. They told her to untie Eugene and never mention their presence.

Eugene heard the female voice and cried out, "Help me, please!"

"Just a minute, sir." As Mandy untied Eugene, he took the pillowcase off.

"Did you see anyone?"

"No, sir, I didn't." Mandy tried to keep a straight face. She realized that this guest had wet and soiled his pants, and he was shaking something awful. "Sir, if I see any suspicious activity, I will report it to the police."

"Thank you, young lady." Eugene quickly took the coffee and ushered Mandy out of the room.

The red-haired, freckled, clumsy teen was only too glad to get away from the malodorous guest. Eugene drank the coffee and undressed. He cleaned himself as best he could. The soiled underwear he washed in the sink and discarded. He reshowered and lay down on his bed. As he hit the pillow, he heard something ruffle; he felt underneath it. It was a letter. Eugene quickly grabbed the letter and read it.

Eugene Balkner. You have ruffled the feathers of the main body of Scotland.

If we hear any more reports of you abandoning our principles of waiting for God to come to our aid in crafting a pure society, you will not see our next generation of fellow members blossom. This isn't a threat, Eugene. It's a promise.

Consider yourself suspended. Stay away from any Sheppard activity for six months. Any trouble you may have, you handle yourself. That's an order, not a request.

—The Sheppards

Eugene put the letter down. He couldn't believe how one black man could cause so much trouble. Now he was barred from contacting his fellow Sheppards. He would still pay the men who had done the deed for him, he promised himself. He could do that if he could just find them. For the moment, going back to Philly wouldn't be too smart. Maybe he'd try Oregon. A business partner there could put him up for a while.

May 2001 was not turning out too well for Hank Albright. He decided to speak with Erwin Borghorst, who's been a state senator for eight years. He was a straight shooter who was elected because of his integrity. Albright knew the senator would at least listen to him. The detective patiently waited in the senator's office, reading a magazine. The receptionist came into the lobby. "Sir, the senator will see you now,"

"Thank you."

The senator had tried to gather as much information on Albright as possible before this meeting. The detective appeared to have information that was damning, or he wanted to discuss a dirty cop. The senator learned that Albright was a good lawman, and that he'd recently been involved in a shooting.

"What can I do for you, detective?"

"Well sir, I'm in a bit of jam. I was hoping you could help me."

"I'm a busy man, Detective Albright, but tell me what's on your mind."

Well, sir, do you know anything about a group called the Sheppards?" Borghorst was quiet and considerate. He had known about the Sheppards for some time. They had been instrumental in getting him elected. They were an influential group, indeed. "What about the Sheppards, detective?"

"Well, senator, we've had some trouble . . ."

Borghorst cut Albright off. "The shooting, detective?"

"Yes, senator." Albright's hopes brightened.

Senator Borghorst knew that the detective was a fly in the ointment. "Look, detective, you write a report, and give it to me, and I'll see what I can do for you. That sound reasonable?" Albright felt that he could trust the senator. "I'll do that, senator, right away."

"Good." The senator stood up and shook hands with Albright. "Oh, and detective, I'd keep things under wraps. You don't want any ugly rumors to spread. That clear?"

Albright got a sinking feeling. "Yes, senator, I understand." Albright was trembling as he walked out of the lobby.

Chu convinced me to stay in Seattle. On the night that we were to leave, Chu said, "Look, my friend, lay low with me for a couple of days. You'll be protected."

I was devastated over the breakup with Casey. All I could do was relive the memories of love and togetherness. Casey was thirteen years my senior, but she had turned me into a man. I had felt so secure with my lady, and now she was gone.

"Roger!"

"Sure, Chu. I'm game."

"Great. Let's go to my place and get something to eat."

Even though I wasn't hungry, I didn't argue. When we arrived at Chu's home in upscale Seattle, I was impressed. I had never been near Chu's home or in this part of the city. "Damn, Chu, you live right up there with the best of them!"

"Roger, I just take what the man will give me. I'm a flea on the horse's back. I could be squashed any minute, so, my friend, I choose to live while I can."

I nodded. I had the $3,000 that Casey had given me, and I knew full well that Chu would not let me spend too much money. I would have to call my family in Utah. No doubt they were worried about me.

Casey and Anne were on the freeway, getting as far away from Seattle they could before they stopped to rest. Behind the wheel, Casey was reflecting on her life. She had loved Roger more because of the stark contrast between them than anything else. Roger was a young, ambitious man. He might have been involved in some illegal activity, yet she respected him for his discretion in the matter. Casey looked over at her mother, who was fast asleep. She felt good that her mother had finally taken a stand against her father. Their family would never be the same. Casey concentrated on her next move. She planned to get in touch with Allen and take him up on his offer. It probably wouldn't work out, but what the hell. There were plenty of fish in the sea, even if some were of a different species.

Her father was a man possessed—Casey was sure of it. Why else would he behave so erratically? If he could have accepted Roger, everything would have been okay. Casey couldn't help but be saddened over the calamity that had just played out in her life. Eugene would always be her father, and even though she resented him, Casey still felt the love that she had for her dad. She turned off the freeway on the outskirts of Idaho. She and her mom needed to rest and plan their strategy.

Alfredo

CHAPTER 15

LOS ANGELES

Alfredo made it to Brantley's Garage in Trenton. He had become nauseated by Snook's body odor. Alfredo was going to insist that Snook take a shower.

Don Parillo was away on business, but he had left the arrangements with Joey Stein, a Jewish wannabe. A one-armed man with fire in his eyes, Joey had lost his left arm in a gang war in Harlem, back in 1983. He was known to have killed over eleven men. His arm had become infected and had to be amputated at the bicep. Joey was still very formidable with his strong right arm.

"Hey, Joey, what's shakin'?" Alfredo was pretending to be glad to see his antagonist. "Don Parillo sends you his love, boy!" Joey didn't like Alfredo, but he respected Don Parillo's judgment.

"I love, you too, Joey!"

"Here's the information from Mr. Parillo." Alfredo took the brown 81/2-by-11 envelope, which was extremely full, touched Joey's stump, smiled, and looked around the garage. Only the mechanics were here at this hour. Pretty soon, at around 10:00 a.m., the place would be crawling with people doing everything from fixing limousines to selling drugs and loaning money. Alfredo was amazed at the number of people who borrowed at the interest rate Parillo was charging. Sure, he had bone breakers to collect the money, but why borrow from underworld characters? Alfredo would never understand the psychology of the little guy.

As they drove from Parillo's, Alfredo had had enough, so he decided to say something. "Mack, your boy is going to have to clean up. Damn!"

Mack started laughing hysterically and finally straightened up. "Yeah, man, ole Snook really offends people, but he's a hell of a man; he'll battle with you to the end!"

Snook finally spoke up. "Look, Alfredo, I need a change of clothes too. I been out on the streets for five days, and I been hard up for everything."

"We'll go by my place, and you can clean up there. I'll let you use my washing machine and dryer. That should help." Alfredo sped home, then ushered both Mack and Snook into his apartment. The apartment smelled of rotting garbage and exhaust, but it was pure oxygen, considering that Alfredo had spent the last ten minutes cooped up in his car with the foul-smelling Snook.

Alfredo wasn't about to waste money buying Snook clothes. Snook could wash and dry his clothes here and then they would leave for California.

Alfredo led both men to his room and told them to undress, take a shower, and then wash their filthy rags. Both of them were dressed ragged, but that would have to do. Alfredo was grateful that he had a place to stay and clean himself.

While his crew changed their soiled white T-shirts and worn and tattered dungarees, Alfredo opened the envelope he had gotten from Don Parillo, and checked its contents. There was at least $20,000 inside, plus a map leading to a private airport in Newark. Alfredo chuckled at Don's thoroughness. Alfredo leaned back in his chair; his brown slacks and retro-style brown shirt would last him for several days. He'd take as little as possible on the trip. Wearing clothes for several days wouldn't be a problem. The smell came with the territory. Alfredo made the three of them salami-and-cheese sandwiches. He ate his and took a nap.

Several hours later the men were aboard a small, private jet, headed to Los Angeles. Snook finally smelled like a civilized person. Mack had fallen asleep shortly after takeoff. Alfredo sensed that this was the pair's first flight. Alfredo had flown several times doing other jobs for the family. As the jet roared toward Los Angeles, Alfredo wondered what the future held for them.

Alfredo jumped up at the jarring sensation he felt. He had been asleep for over an hour. He looked at his watch; they'd left New Jersey over three hours ago. As the three men disembarked from the aircraft at a private Santa Monica airport, there were two men on the landing strip waiting for them—Parillo's men.

Alfredo bristled at Parillo's power. Then he wondered why Parillo had chosen him for the job. Why didn't he just get one of his high-priced hit men? Alfredo was brought back to reality by one of the men, who said, "Who are these two?"

"These are my boys. They're in this up to here." Alfredo pointed to his neck and then ran his finger across it.

Parillo's men, both dressed in tailor-made, dark-blue suits, and alligator shoes, didn't flinch, which made a good impression on Alfredo. He recalled the sharp-dressing Don Parillo, who always sported a suit. Both of these men were well built, with the leader apparently the one asking the questions. He was the one who motioned for Alfredo to follow them. Alfredo gestured to Mack and Snook to tag along. They followed the men outside the airport to a decent-looking, used, blue Chevy Impala. It was an inconspicuous car that probably wouldn't draw too much attention from the police.

"Take this car and use it for whatever you need it for, capeesh?"

"Got ya!" Alfredo felt right at home with the two gentlemen.

"Thanks, boys. I owe you one."

Both men broke into mischievous laughter, saying, "You'll pay soon enough, fella!"

The men pointed to the exit and quietly walked away. Alfredo watched the two well-built men leave. They could have passed for actors.

Alfredo got a pleasant feeling in his loins thinking of the women those two no doubt got plenty of. It had been a long time since Alfredo had had a woman. The last one was his fourteen-year-old sister. Alfredo knew that they had different fathers and also that she was one hot momma, but his conscience always seemed to eat at him. He had sex with her three times, and he had planned to keep at it, but the shred of decency left in him continually gnawed at him. Taking her virginity still haunted him. The last time she slipped into his room naked, Alfredo kissed her and sent her away promising he'd do it later. She giggled, stroked Alfredo's penis, and went back into her room.

Alfredo was jolted back to reality by Mack. "Let's get out of here, yo. I'm getting nervous. Who're these people you're working for?"

"Just a man, Mack, just a man." Alfredo got into the car and cranked it up. "Pure fire here, boys!"

The Impala was in mint condition; it was a '93, yet it had the feel of a new car. Alfredo wheeled the smooth-running vehicle out of the small airport. The guards seemed to care very little about the car; they turned their backs as Alfredo drove by.

Cruising by Santa Monica Bay, he got on his cell phone and called T-Bone. This time, once Alfredo identified himself, T-Bone came right on the line, saying, "What's up, Alfie? Are you in LA?"

"Yeah, bro, I arrived a little ahead of schedule."

"Are you rolling?"

"Yeah, I've got a clean Chevy, probably a 350 under the hood, and this bitch is legit, too!"

"Where are you?"

Alfredo hesitated before answering, "I'm at an airport in Santa Monica."

"Well, get ready for a ride!"

"I'm ready, T-Bone!"

"Okay, hit the 10 and travel until you get to the 405, and let it lead you in."

"Gotcha, T-Bone!" Alfredo headed for the freeway. He was amazed at the complexity of the roadways in California.

Finally, after two hours, he made it to the place where he was meeting T-Bone. Alfredo was tense, sweaty, and somewhat disoriented. Mack and Snook were stone silent. They had never witnessed such a maze. They waited well over an hour before a young black man in a red jumpsuit and gold chains approached them, saying, "You, Alfie?"

Alfredo instantly knew the boy had been sent by T-Bone. Alfredo tried to keep his composure after smelling the foul breath of the raggedy-toothed teenager. "Yeah, I'm Alfredo. Where's T-Bone?"

"Follow me," the kid said. Alfredo watched the boy walk away and disappear into a shiny, black Mercedes, probably a '99. Alfredo started the engine and began following the Mercedes. He drove past some hellish sights. Abandoned buildings, burned-out property. Alfredo knew poverty, and this was an area in dire straits. Alfredo winced as he observed the barricaded houses. The place looked like a war zone. The characters who patrolled the streets were dangerous-looking men. As the Mercedes pulled into a driveway, Alfredo parked on the street. He, Mack, and Snook cautiously got out of the Impala. A man walked toward them from inside the house. A tall, slender, brown-skinned man, stylish and good-looking, except for his kinky afro, he could have passed for a famous rapper. Alfredo finally recognized him.

"T-Bone. Boy, it's been a long time!" Alfredo shouted.

"Alfie!" The two men embraced tightly. "Alfie, you did well getting here, man. Most people would have gotten lost as hell!"

"I learned in Jersey, T-Bone. But, damn, LA is one twisted mutha!"

"You know it, too. I get lost trying to go to the store." Both men laughed heartily at T-Bone's wry sense of humor. T-Bone ushered the three men into his home. It was a stark contrast to the battleground outside. It was very well-kept and decorated very nicely. "Like my place, Alfie?" T-Bone asked.

Alfredo nodded his head in approval. This home, modest in size, looked like a three-bedroom affair. Soft, pleasant music filled the living room. Despite how the three of them were dressed, T-Bone still offered, "You guys want to go to a party with me?"

Alfredo spoke for the three of them. "Sure, T-Bone. Where's the gig?"

"It's over at one of my girl's place. It's just for players you know what I mean?"

"I know what you mean, T-Bone, but why are you inviting us?"

Alfredo felt a little out of place, since he knew how players operated.

"Hey, Alfie, it's just a few of us getting together. What do you say?"

"Shit, why not. I need to loosen up a bit." T-Bone motioned over to his guy, saying, "Yuck Mouth, get the car ready for me and my boys."

"Sure, Bone, I'm on it." As Yuck Mouth went out to get the car, Alfredo asked, "Why do you call him Yuck Mouth, T-Bone?"

"Cause he has halitosis, and his breath smells like shit!" Alfredo laughs so hard that T-Bone had to tell him to take it easy. As they headed out to the car, Alfredo was concerned about the Impala in this neighborhood. "Will my car be okay, Bone?"

"Yeah, man, no one touches anything near my place, solid?"

"Solid, Bone!" Alfredo motioned for Mack and Snook to get in the back seat with him. As Yuck Mouth drove, T-Bone began explaining things to Alfredo. "Look, Alfie, I remember telling you in the joint that I would get mine, and look at me now!"

"Yeah, I see, T-Bone. How much you doin' now, my man?"

"I distribute now. I don't need to do street slanging. I'm at the top of my game. Man, I distribute to all of California by making a few phone calls to my runners, and they do all the work."

"How'd you manage that?" Alfredo was truly impressed with the professional way T-Bone handled his business. "Well, Alfie, I worked my way to the top. As you know, LA is a mecca for drugs. You have to know the right people. If you don't, you could easily be taken out. I have the whole area of Watts watching my back. I can go anywhere, and nobody will mess with me. Not because I'm tough, but because, without me, drugs won't move."

"Well, T-Bone, you certainly have done well for yourself." Alfredo wanted to ask about Chu, but decided to give it some time. He didn't want to step on any toes.

"Gentlemen, welcome to my playhouse!"

Alfredo had been so immersed in the story of T-Bone's life that he let everything get by him. He had no idea where they were or how they'd gotten there.

Mack and Snook were way out of their element. They were petty hustlers. They didn't know how to relate with the heavyweights. Alfredo didn't want to needle them or insist that they make small talk. The inside of the car smelled of Yuck Mouth. When T-Bone insisted that everyone get out, go inside, and see how the West Coast got it on, Alfredo could see that this area was as stripped of decency as T-Bone's territory.

When they entered the home, Alfredo was pleasantly surprised. There were at least six voluptuous young black women there in their bras and panties. T-Bone smiled at Alfredo's reaction. "A little something for my boy. Hey, Alfie, none of this would be possible if it weren't for you so, my friend, take your pleasure!"

"Don't worry, T-Bone, I will definitely take you up on that!" Both men laughed heartily at the knowledge of the highest form of pleasure known to man. Mack and Snook grabbed two women each and began groping them. The women led both men into the rear of the sparsely decorated den of sex.

Alfredo, still wanting to communicate with T-Bone, just stood there. "What are you waiting for Alfie? Jump right in!"

"In time, my friend, in time. Tell me something, T-Bone, what's the catch?"

"Alfie, I'm surprised at you. There is no catch." T-Bone sized Alfredo up. He had grown over the years. Alfredo was a dangerous man, capable of killing even a skilled soldier with his bare hands if he got close enough. Whoever had sent Alfie out here wanted results. T-Bone was a cautious man. You don't become a major player without watching your back. He'd just wait and see. For now he wanted to relax his protégé a little bit. He might even tell T-Bone's girls something.

"Mae!"

"What you want, nigga?"

"Hey, woman, just come here!" Mae walked over to T-Bone and Alfie. "Alfie, Mae is my housekeeper; she'll take care of you. I'll be back in a couple of days and pick you guys up." T-Bone motioned for Yuck Mouth, and both men quietly left.

"Hello, lady," Alfredo said.

"Hey, man, what's your name, cutie?" Mae came closer, rubbing Alfredo's scar in the process.

Alfredo took her hand and kissed it. "My name's Alfredo, babe."

"Well, Alfredo, what can Mae do for you?"

"Girl, I want some lovin', to tell you the truth."

"Let's go in my room and get comfortable."

"Okay, babe." Alfredo's erection was almost painful now. He'd gone without sex for a long time, yet now he was so near that he let go of all restraint. Mae led Alfredo into a small neatly kept room.

"This is my playpen, sugar." Alfredo felt he was really going to like this. The two shared a long, passionate kiss. As he held the soft and sensual Mae tightly in his arms, Alfredo felt himself climax. He grabbed Mae tightly and pressed hard against her as the fluid exquisitely spewed out. Alfredo had had premature ejaculations before, but this one was so powerful that Alfredo went down on his knees.

"What's wrong sweetheart?" Alfredo was silent.

Mae saw what had happened and said, "Am I to much for you, Alfredo, babe?"

"Girl, I saw all that pretty skin, and I just couldn't hold it!"

Both Alfredo and Mae quickly began to undress. The sex was the wild-animal, passionate kind—rough and hard—but Alfredo liked it that way. He had to take it easy on his little sister, something he'd never had gotten used to. Mae was all woman: She could easily accommodate the large and deep-thrusting Alfredo.

The next morning, Alfredo awoke at around 8:00 a.m. Mae wasn't there, but Alfredo felt good after a night's tussle with her. She appeared in the doorway. "You feel like eating, Alfredo?"

"Sure, girl. I'm starved." Alfredo got out of bed and tried to dress.

"Hey, Alfredo, let's take a shower together." Alfredo eagerly agreed, saying, "Alright, girl. I could use a cleanup."

"I'll put your clothes in the washer. They need some freshening up."

"That sounds good. Thanks." As both Alfredo and Mae cleaned up that morning, everyone else, including Mack and Snook, had already eaten and washed and gotten back into their pleasure modes. Alfredo was dressed, he'd eaten, and now he wanted to relax and have some pillow talk with Mae. As he lay on the bed, Mae stroked him and said, "Are you staying in LA?"

"I plan on being around a few days. I have some business to take care of."

"What kind of business, Alfie. Can I come along?"

"Aren't you T-Bone's girl?"

"Yeah, but I want to be my own person. T-Bone takes good care of me, but it gets kind of boring, if you know what I mean."

"I think I understand, but at least you're safe."

"Maybe. Anyway, how do you know T-Bone?"

"I was locked up with him in New York. We became friends."

"Oh, so you knew T-Bone from the old school?"

"You could say that. We go way back."

"You plan on working with T-Bone?"

"Well, Mae, I just want to see if T-Bone could give me some information on someone."

"Well, T-Bone is large, so take it easy."

"I should be okay, Mae." Mae was looking into Alfredo's eyes. She sort of liked him. He sure knew how to plunge in and out of her. His forcefulness caused her to have multiple orgasms. Mae kissed Alfredo. They began thrashing around on the bed, and were soon ready to repeat last night's performance.

When T-Bone came to pick the boys up, they were all ready to leave. Having a one-night stand was one thing, but nonstop sex for two days has a tendency to make a man tuck tail and run. Alfredo said his good-byes to Mae. Alma, who didn't get to sleep with anyone, gave all three men a kiss. She squeezed Alfredo's groin as he left the house, saying, "Take it easy, big boy!"

"I will, sugar, and keep it hot for me, love."

T-Bone ushered the three men into the Mercedes. On the trip back, all of them were silent. T-Bone thought he'd let Alfie contemplate things. He wanted to know why Alfie had come to Los Angeles and who he was looking for. They arrived at T-Bone's home, and went inside. T-Bone had softened Alfie up enough.

"Hey, Alfie, I know you and the way you work. Maybe I can help you."

"Yeah, maybe you can, T-Bone. Do you know Won Chu?"

T-Bone almost choked, but kept his composure. Won Chu was the supplier for most of the West Coast. Even though Chu didn't generally deal directly, he ran the Chinese syndicate. T-Bone cleared his throat. "Alfie, you're into some hard shit. Won Chu—why him?"

"I'm just a scout. The man I work for—one of his people was iced, and he's curious. Won Chu's name popped up."

"So what did you bring your two bodyguards for?" T-Bone disrespectfully eyed Mack and Snook, who said nothing.

"They are my eyes and ears, T-Bone."

"Well, Won Chu lives in Seattle, and he has a lot of people backing him up. You don't have enough juice to handle him. I feel for you, but damn! Whoever sent you didn't know squat—Chu is a firecracker, man! You can find him in the red-light district."

T-Bone wouldn't lie to him, and he felt that he might be in over his head, but Alfredo did promise Don Parillo that he'd check into it, so he would.

"Anything else I can do for you, Alfie?"

"No, you've done plenty. I owe you, big man."

"No, Alfie, I still say my prayers thinking of the time they tried to rearrange my anus in the joint!" Everyone laughed long and hard at that one. T-Bone composed himself. "Yuck, bring some drinks!"

"Alright, Boss." T-Bone was watching Alfredo, who returned the stare. T-Bone broke it, saying, "Alfie, you've always been the man in my book. Why don't you stay here and work for me?"

"Let me take care of my business, and I'll get back at you, solid?"

"Solid, Alfie. I'll be in touch."

Alfredo stood up and motioned for Mack and Snook to follow him. He embraced T-Bone and walked out. The Impala was untouched. All three men got into the Impala and headed away from T-Bone's. Alfredo knew he could never find the place again, even if he wanted too. He headed out of Watts, trying to get back to Santa Monica. He had a phone call to make.

T-Bone was puzzled. Alfie was a legitimate friend, but Chu was his bread and butter. He'd worked with Chu for over four years. Not that he was crazy for him, but it was a matter of principle. Alfie was an outsider, and he worked for the East Coast family. T-Bone's runners in Tacoma had told him about the Italian who tried to muscle two hundred pounds of smack out of the Chinese syndicate. T-Bone shook his head. He had one hundred pounds of the stuff in circulation. He didn't want to rat out Alfie, so he wouldn't make the call to Seattle.

Skipper

CHAPTER 16

SEATTLE

Alfredo was deep in thought as he pondered his next move. They found a room off Santa Monica Boulevard. He called the number that the family had given him. He was told to go to Seattle and find Chu. A black man named Skipper would guide Alfredo to Seattle and possibly find some of the thugs who hustled in the area.

Alfredo, Mack, and Snook were recovering from their liaisons in a single room. Mack had been soaking up everything they'd been through. Now was the time for Mack to speak up. "You know, Alfredo, me and Snook have enjoyed being with you, but, my man, what are we going to do when we get to Seattle?"

Alfredo, a pleasant look on his face thinking of Mae, answered his protégé. "All I want you to do is be my eyes and ears, Mack."

Mack had been doing a lot of thinking, and he wanted out. He knew when he was in over his head. "Look, Alfredo, me and Snook have been thinking and, to be honest, we're scared, man."

Alfredo had been thinking along the same lines. Mack and Snook were a hindrance; they just weren't the type to be able to handle men like Chu. T-Bone must have really frightened them. Mack was right; maybe he should just send them home to Jersey. Alfredo figured he'd give them bus fare and $200 each. Now was the best time for them to back out. Otherwise, Alfredo would have killed them.

"Okay, Mack. I'll call a cab, and you and Snook can get the bus back to Jersey."

Mack had been a hustler for many years, and he knew when to call it quits. Snook would do whatever he said. Mack was amused that Snook, who hardly spoke at all, had whispered to Mack that he wanted to go home. Mack was grateful for the women; they had really made this trip worthwhile. Then Snook, who had been silent the whole time, went over to Alfredo and said, "It's been a stone gas, hanging out with you man, but you are after big game, man. I'm just small fry."

"I understand, Snook. I'll see you in Jersey." They shook hands and laughed about their romp with the ladies. Alfredo sat on the bed, turned on the medium-sized television, and waited for things to happen. Mack and Snook prepared to leave.

Skipper arrived three hours later. Mack and Snook had been gone for a couple of hours already. They had taken the money gratefully and headed back east.

Skipper was a short, squat man, with a deep voice, powerful arms, and pointy eyebrows. He looked like a small pirate without the sword. He was a felon from Chino who had served twelve years for kidnapping and robbery, a job he'd did for the family over eight years ago. Skipper, whose real name was Melvin Jones, had been sent to help Alfredo with anything he needed. Alfredo liked Skipper, who was a hard man—someone Alfredo could count on.

"Hey, Alfredo, you ready to hit the highway, man?"

"Let's get a bite to eat first. I'm starved." Both men agreed, and Alfredo checked out of the hotel some six hours after he'd checked in. His weapons and money were in the overnight bag in the Impala. Skipper put his belongings in the trunk, then suggested that he do the driving. "I know the territory, so why don't you let me drive, okay?"

"Sounds good to me," said Alfredo, as he held out the keys to the Impala.

"We'll get a quick bite at one of the local fast food places, Alfredo."

"Right now I could eat the back side of a mule's ass. Anywhere is fine with me."

"We'll go to this joint I know called Mabelene's. It's good food, and it's fast." As Skipper started the Impala, he was impressed. "Now this here is ready for the road, Alfredo. We're in business!"

"Yeah, she really purrs," Alfredo added. Mabelene's was a nice, out-of-the way place without too many customers. Alfredo respected Skipper for his insight.

T-Bone had been restless ever since Alfredo left. He'd done his friend a huge favor by letting him pleasure the whores T-Bone kept for himself. No one except Yuck Mouth and a few others were allowed there, and, to top it off, Alfredo had balled Mae, T-Bone's top girl. T-Bone had bought Mae from a local crack dealer named Mud, who sold her for two ounces of smack. The sale was illegal, but he knew that Mae would respect him for making such a move. After the sale, Mae vowed to be loyal to T-Bone, and she'd been with him for two years. She had moved from Compton after the sale. Alfredo was the first besides T-Bone to be with her.

Now T-Bone was deciding whether or not to give Chu a heads-up. T-Bone wasn't a snitch, but Chu was a big-league player, who handled the purchases of smack T-Bone made from that territory.

T-Bone had grown to love Alfredo. Even though they rarely spoke, T-Bone would never forget that Alfredo spared him a brutal experience. T-Bone had heard and witnessed the wrecking of many anuses by desperate male predators. T-Bone finally decided to let Alfredo and Chu handle their own affairs. If Alfredo managed to take Chu out, then Chu must be slipping. No, T-Bone wouldn't touch this one.

After picking up a fifth of Jim Beam, Alfredo and Skipper headed toward Seattle. When they hit Oakland some six hours later, Skipper wanted to buy some expensive weed, and he knew of a dealer in Oakland's flatlands who would gladly sell his prison buddy several ounces of cannabis. As Skipper got near the dealer's place of business, two young men in dark clothes and backwards baseball caps approached the Impala with their hands on their weapons, shouting, "What's up, nigga?"

Skipper was unfazed by the two, booming out, "Hey, look, homey, I need to contact Dee Tee—we go way back. Matter of fact, we go back to the lockup in Chino!"

"You know Dee Tee from Chino?"

"Yeah. I'm Skipper."

"Shit, homey, in a minute."

Dee Tee came out, putting away his cell phone and smashing a cigarette on the banged-up sidewalk. "Skipper! Nigga, what's up? Been a long time, my boy!"

"Dee Tee! No thang but a chicken wang!"

The men went through their prison ritual of the prison dap and high five. They had met each other doing time and were released on the same day. They had exchanged addresses and vowed to stay in touch. Skipper got the West Coast family to use Dee Tee as a runner. Dee Tee had a lot of homeys working and could bring in serious money for the family. Dee Tee was accountable for over $3 million a year. Most of it went to the family.

As the men relaxed a little, Skipper checked out his partner. Dee Tee hadn't changed over the years. Still tall and lanky, but his face was a little coarser. Still the playboy, Dee Tee was half-Indian with hair down to his shoulders—was naturally curly and shiny black. He was a well-formed man. Skipper remembered Dee Tee's indiscretions in the joint when he'd let the homosexuals give him oral sex. Dee Tee promised he wouldn't do it on the outside—he was just blowing off steam while in the joint. Skipper couldn't care less, as long as Dee Tee didn't look at him sideways. Skipper bought two ounces of fine northern California hemp.

"This shit is for real, Skipper. You better not drive and smoke this shit!"

"Hey, man, I could smoke Sherm and handle myself on the highway."

"Who's your boy sitting over there all by himself in that sweet Impala?"

"That's Alfredo. We're doing a job in Seattle. We'll be back through in a week or so."

"Seattle, what's so hot up there?"

"Drugs and money, Dee Tee, drugs and money!" The two men embraced and punched each other hard in the chest. Skipper walked back to the car with the weed, cranked up the engine, and he and Alfredo headed out before the cops came. The Impala drove like a hand running through silk. Once on Interstate-5, they would take it to Oregon and then up to Seattle. Skipper stopped at a cheap motel on the outskirts of San Francisco and rolled at least twenty joints. Alfredo couldn't believe that Skipper could smoke and drive. Alfredo smoked two, but was so paranoid that he decided to leave the shit alone after that. He had smoked some good weed in his time, but that smoke was the best he ever had.

Seattle was the Emerald City. For now, though, Skipper had business to take care of. Skipper knew several niggers who lived there, and he figured that they had connections through the dope game. Emerald City or not, they weren't on a pleasure trip. Skipper spoke first. "Look, Alfredo, I'm going to put the word out that we're looking for some smack. Then we'll sit back and see what happens."

"Sounds like a plan, man!"

Skipper then called Tick Williams. Tick made a living snitching back and forth to underworld characters and working as a front for the dealers. Skipper knew he was on the take to the highest bidder.

"Hello. Who is this?"

"This is Skipper from Compton."

"What you need?"

"Look, man, I need two pounds of smack. Where can I get it from?"

"You come down to the central part of the city, and meet me at Jefferson Street. And bring $20,000."

"Damn, nigga, why so much?"

"Hey, look, I'm doing you a favor. Either we do business or we don't—understand?"

"Okay, okay, take it easy."

"Be there at 2:30 in the morning. It's 11:30 now, so wait a few hours, solid?"

"I gotcha. I'll be there." It was Tuesday, May 11. Skipper wanted this shit over within two days. He looked at Alfredo, who seemed stoned.

"You okay, Alfredo? Man, you looked whipped!"

"I'm alright. Just let me know when we get to the action."

"Well, I'm driving over to Jefferson Street to wait for Tick there. We can rest once we get there."

"Sounds good, Skipper. In the meantime, I need a nap."

Skipper headed for Jefferson Street.

By 2:00 a.m. Tick had been calling all over Seattle trying to find two pounds of smack. Finally, Tick reached a Chinese guy named Cheng, and told him that he had a customer who wanted two pounds of smack. Cheng got hold of Chu's people, who told Chu. Chu had been enjoying his visit with me for a week or so. He hadn't done any dealing, figuring he could take it easy. It had been a pleasure for him to learn all about my life. My romantic interludes with Casey had really excited Chu. Chu exclaimed, "Roger, you are going to have to quit telling me these steamy stories, or I'll have an accident!"

"Quit it, Chu," I teased. The phone call interrupted us. It was Cheng.

"Hey, Chu, I have someone who wants an order. You game?"

"I might be. What's the deal?"

"Well, meet Tick at Jefferson Street. That's where the buyers'll be."

"How can I get in touch with Tick beforehand?" Chu asked

"I'll give you his number."

Chu knew about Tick. He was a businessman all right, yet you had to stay on your toes in dealing with him—he could be as venomous as a rattler. Tick answered his cell phone.

"This is Chu. Tell me, what's the deal?"

"I need two pounds by 2:30. Can you deliver?"

"Yeah, I can deliver. What part of Jefferson?"

"By the medical center. I'll be in a red Volkswagen right around the corner, Chu."

"Meet you there." Chu looked over at me. "You feel like making some money, my friend?"

"I could sure use some, Chu."

"Well, let me get my stuff ready, and I'll meet you in the van." Chu went into his garage where he kept sometimes up to five pounds of smack. This would be an easy job.

Tick got back in touch with Skipper. "Hey, man," Tick said. "Me and a guy named Chu are going to be there in about twenty minutes. What are you driving?"

"We'll be in a blue Chevy Impala, waiting."

"Good!" Click. Skipper felt his blood heating up. Here was Chu, right in their fingertips. "Hey, wake up, Alfredo! Guess what? Chu's coming right to us. We just got to wait here." Skipper went to the trunk and checked his money. He had $50,000, so he took out five stacks and shut the trunk. The two men shared a joint while they waited. Skipper decided to call in to tell his people that they were in close contact with Chu.

Skipper was sure that they'd want him to ice Chu right away and get back, but the order was to make sure that Chu had the stuff. The missing smack was 80 percent pure. Just get the smack, check it, and report back to us, Skipper's contact said. Skipper was disappointed. "Come all this way to buy some damn heroin. Damn!" He told Alfredo. Both men were a bit gloomy and almost didn't notice the light-colored van pull up next to them. Both Chu and I were armed. Chu spoke first.

"You Skipper?"

"Who wants to know?"

"Hey, I'm looking for Skipper. If you're not him, I'll see you later." Chu put the van in gear.

"Hold it, man! Yeah, I'm Skipper, and I want to deal."

Chu parked the van a few feet away from the Impala. Tick was in the back seat of the van. He vaguely recognized Skipper, but he couldn't be sure where he knew him from. Tick didn't want to think about this too long or hard. All he wanted was the $2,000 Chu was going to give him.

Chu got out of the van and cautiously approached the Impala. Alfredo squinted, trying to get a good look at Chu. My hand on my trusty revolver, I slid out of the vehicle. All of a sudden Tick's memory kicked in. He remembered that Skipper was a member of the West Coast family. Through the grapevine he knew that Skipper was a professional.

"Chu! Wait a minute!" Tick shouted.

As Skipper and Alfredo realized what was happening, they both went for their weapons. But Chu had the upper hand.

"Just stay where you are, boys!"

Chu had his sights trained on the men. I quickly stepped away from the van, cocked my revolver, and went to the front of the Impala.

Both Alfredo and Skipper knew that they were at the mercy of Chu and his boys. Skipper rationalized that the booze and drugs had affected his own and Alfredo's catlike reflexes.

Then, thinking fast, Skipper said, "Look, fellas, all we want is some smack!"

"Who sent you?" Chu demanded angrily.

Alfredo spoke up. "Take it easy, man. We're looking for our drugs—that's all!"

"What drugs?" Chu pointed his weapon menacingly at both men.

"Well, if you want to know, Gillione's drugs."

Chu saw it all fall in place. Gillione didn't do the crimes, yet Chu knew exactly who did. "Well, boys, your man Gillione tried to steal from us."

Skipper feigned sympathy. "Well, I just want two pounds of drugs!"

Tick's blunder could have caused a shootout; he humbly sat down in the back seat of the van.

"Roger get that smack out and bring it over here!" I realized that Chu had the drop on these two, and fished the heroin out of the van. I handed it to Tick and then trained my thirty-eight on Alfredo. Alfredo sat deathly still.

"Where's the money?" Chu asked, as he aimed his .357 at Skipper's head.

Skipper said, "It's right here, man. Take it easy!" He slowly brought out the cash.

Chu motioned for Tick to hand over the drugs and take the money. Tick nimbly complied.

Chu eyed the two men. "Gentlemen, you are welcome to do business with me, but don't come to me crying about fair play. Now get outta here!"

Skipper turned on the ignition and mulled over his next move for a few seconds. Should I ram them? He thought better of it and guided the Impala away from them. He and Alfredo both knew that they could have been fish bait.

"Damn, Alfredo, we just about paid the piper on that one." Skipper called his people in Los Angeles.

Lorenzo Bolino had gotten word about Alfredo's mission from Don Parillo. Parillo knew that Gillione was a man who pushed people too far. Parillo loved his friend, and he wanted to know what happened.

When Skipper called, Lorenzo gave him further instructions: "We want you and Alfredo to be our main men in Washington. Go to Tacoma—North 46th Street—and find Jimmy's Plumbing. Talk to Enzo Oliva. He'll be waiting for you." Lorenzo then hung up.

Skipper thought about the brief conversation, and then turned to Alfredo, saying, "Hey, man, they want us to be distributors."

Alfredo never imagined that Don Parillo would use him this way, but he was in so deep now, that if he didn't do it he'd be a wanted man. Alfredo thought about his mother and his sisters. Maybe he could get in touch with them and visit every so often. He thought about Mack and Snook and how they had weaseled out of things. Alfredo saw his life flash before him. He was family property.

"Well, Skipper, I'm always up for a challenge. Where are we headed?"

Skipper looked at Alfredo, smiled, and said, "Let's hit it, 'cause we in it to win it!" Skipper lit a joint and then made a call to Oakland.

Casey

CHAPTER 17

THE TRIP

Casey felt so safe in Allen's arms. She loved Roger, but, to be honest, that was more passion than love. With Allen she could let go and be the little girl she always wanted to be. "Allen, why do people hate each other so much?"

Allen enjoyed Casey's company. She had totally surprised him by coming back to Cleveland to be with him. They spent their first night together tonight. Casey was a little out of sync at first. She was used to being with a rambunctious youngster like Roger, but after several of Allen's reassuring pecks on the cheek, she calmed down. The two of them felt as if they belonged together. Casey would remember Roger for a long time, but she was having fun learning about her new love, Allen.

Anne felt free for the first time in years. She hadn't realized how restricted she'd been with Eugene. She and Casey rented an apartment not far from Allen Wilson's. She always tried to instill in Casey a love for all people—not just your own kind. Anne remembered a little bit about her escape from Nazi Germany. If it weren't that her father had a substantial amount of money, she would have never gotten out of the prison camps alive. Even though she had only been a child, death was the sentence for all European Jews under the Nazi regime. Few people Anne knew well survived the concentration camps. Anne had heard stories that even money couldn't buy some people a way out. Her father worked for the government and was spirited away by some sympathetic friends. The family barely got out of the country before the roundups began. It was a brutal reminder that hatred unbridled could mean pain and misery not just for the victims, but for the perpetrators as well. Anne remembered well the death camps and the humiliating way she had to live there. For now she was just glad to be her own woman once again. She was meeting a lot of single men in Cleveland.

Chu had gotten me to Utah in three days. We had a terrific time all the way from Seattle. The smoke Chu brought along really made things interesting. Chu had some trouble finding Salt Lake City—Utah was one strange place—but after asking several curious onlookers, Chu finally found his way to Central Utah. Mom was thrilled to see me; she gave me a big hug and cried. She must have held me in her arms for at least fifteen minutes. "Babe, it's so good to see you. I thought we might just have lost you back there in Seattle."

"No, Mom, I was taken good care of by my friends."

Intrigued, Charlotte had to ask. "And just who is big and bad enough to protect you from them folks, son?"

"Well, Mom, my friend Chu here—he can do just about anything."

"He doesn't look like much to me!" Charlotte teased Chu. Then she went over and gave him a big hug. "Both of you come on inside." She was grateful that I hadn't lost my life. She lived in a nice four-bedroom home in central Salt Lake City on Fifth Street. It was a tidy community that Charlotte was proud to live in.

Chu helped me unpack and then he left. "I have to get back right away, Roger. I'll be in touch, my friend!"

"Later, Chu."

Mom began talking about her experiences in Utah. "Roger, I've started my own boutique."

"I'm excited for you, Mom. Maybe I'll be able to help you in some way."

"That would be nice, son. I have been out of rehab for less than a year and I'm already working. Isn't that great?"

"I knew you could do it, Mom. Just hang in there." I was proud of the way things were going for my mother. She had really turned her life around. The sky was the limit.

Daisy and Sonya were now going to a private school in downtown Salt Lake. It was one of the few schools that didn't preach Mormonism. Charlotte wanted to make sure that her girls didn't have the religion pushed on them as she had had in her young years. Daisy still called Pal and wrote to him. It hadn't been long since she had moved to Utah, and the two were already crying and proclaiming their love for each other. Pal promised Daisy that he would save his money and try to come and visit her during the summer.

Dad, having more than enough years at Boeing, put in for his retirement. Boeing had tried to talk him out of it, but he insisted. He wanted to make up for lost time with Charlotte. He was very proud of Charlotte for owning up to her problems and taking charge of her life. He even felt that I would be okay now. Not that he didn't like people of other races, but it was too much trouble for a black man just to be in an interracial relationship.

Theo was still sweet on Charlotte, but he didn't want to admit it. Now that they were here together, Theo's heart had melted away.

I was anxious to meet my new relatives. I had heard my mother lament over the way she had to leave home, and how if she could, she'd find them one day and be a family again.

Now that Mom had reunited with her family, I had a gut feeling that she would kick the habit for good and dedicate herself to taking care of the family.

Her stepfather had died, leaving her mother with enough money to live well. Lou Mary Barns was a giant of a woman. She had been beautiful in her youth. Even though she had gained weight over the years, she still exuded uncanny beauty for a woman her age. She and Charlotte resembled each other so much that they could pass for sisters. Lou loved all her grandchildren. These latest three had captured her heart as well. Now that the family was no longer estranged, she had the opportunity to get to know her eldest daughter and her family. Lou had feared losing Charlotte forever and had prepared herself for it. She was grateful to welcome Charlotte and her family into her life.

Utah was mainly a Caucasian state. It had its share of minorities and while Lou believed in Mormonism, she had drifted away from the church. Lou suspected that the teachings were so whitewashed that a person of color would have to be a genius to figure out her place in church history. Still, some training was better than none.

Her late husband Ralph was such a strict disciplinarian that she never realized how tight a leash he kept her on. She loved Ralph Barns, a burly and good-looking self-made scrap iron dealer who died of natural causes at the age of sixty-three. His death was brought on by exhaustion. The man was a tireless worker. She loved him so much that she was willing to give up on Charlotte years ago when Charlotte walked away from the family. But now, for the first time in her life, she was free to make her own decisions. She would have never forgiven herself if she hadn't seen Charlotte again.

I had gone to Casey's apartment and tried to salvage everything I could. I had called Casey and gotten her address. I had her things shipped to her in Cleveland. It was the least I could do. The episode with the two niggers from Los Angeles had amused me. I hadn't expected people to come looking for Gillione's murderers. Why did they come after Chu? I didn't want to kill anyone, but I was in a game played for keeps. Drugs were big business. People would forever be addicted to illegal drugs, and that heightened my desire for some of the money circulating through the streets.

Albright had been officially suspended. The chief had warned him to keep quiet, and by going to the senator, he had set off a fuse in the department. His only options were to lay low and let whatever was going to happen come to pass. In the meantime, he would keep his hand on his piece. He wasn't going out easy. He hoped Casey and I had taken his advice and left Seattle.

The Sheppard bosses at Sheppard headquarters in Europe were debating how to deal with Eugene Balkner. They had gotten the scoop from Leo Simon. Eugene was completely out of control. His obsession with one "negra" was so petty that the bosses had to be told twice. What would cause a reasonably sharp, self-made man to become overwhelmed with that much anger? Sure, his daughter was balling the bastard, but Eugene had a lot at stake in life and with the Sheppards. For now they hoped the incident at the motel with the pillowcase would bring Eugene to his senses. You can't let one inferior spoil the plans of the Sheppards to rule society from a position of strength.

I was back with my own family. The family had moved in with Charlotte and had begun functioning as a unit once again. It had been a long time. I contemplated my life. I counted myself fortunate to be alive. Life in Utah wouldn't be the same as it was in Seattle. Drug dealing was definitely out. My mother had offered me a job in her boutique, and I was pinching my pennies. Work was the best way to earn a dollar, and I'd do that. But if the opportunity presented itself, I might just go back to dealing drugs.

Six months passed. The family had adjusted, and everyone seemed to like Utah, but we were talking about possibly going back to Seattle. For now, dealing with Utah's unfamiliar culture was the top priority. Daisy and Pal had began to grow apart. I chuckled at such innocence. For the most part, things were going smoothly.

When I found out that Casey was with Allen, I was happy for her. Finding love after all we had gone through was amazing. I was proud of Casey's resilience.

Sonya came to my door, shouting, "Telephone, Roger!"

"Okay, girl, give me the phone," I said. It was Chu.

"Hello, my man, how are you?"

"I'm fine, Chu, what's up?"

"Remember my proposition to you about China?"

"Yes."

"Well, I'm ready to go. When can you meet me?"

"Give me three days."

"Okay, Roger, I'll be waiting. Call me when you get to the airport."

"Okay, Chu. I'll be there."

"See ya!" Damn, I thought Chu had scrapped his plans for China. I had recovered my stash from the Sunbird. Now I would go to China for six months. Eugene Balkner was a distant memory.

Three days later, I was packed and ready to leave. At the dinner table that night, I explained to everyone that I had to go away on for business, but that I'd be back as soon as I could.

I made it to the Seattle-Tacoma Airport a little earlier than I'd planned. Eugene Balkner had flown to Seattle from Oregon the same day. Eugene was pursuing plans to open a store in Seattle again. As he approached the ticket counter, he saw a familiar black face looking at him with intense anger.

"Roger Singleton!" Eugene shouted, as the blood drained from his face.

www.ingramcontent.com/pod-product-compliance
Lightning Source LLC
LaVergne TN
LVHW010215070526
838199LV00062B/4592